He swung her off the ground and headed for the shelter of the veranda

With one arm supporting Leslie's shoulders and the other hooked behind her knees, he fumbled with the keys and finally found the lock.

"Brent?"

He looked down into her wide brown eyes and his hand froze on the knob. "What?"

"Put me down," Leslie whispered. "Please." Her voice caught on the last word and came out in a little sob.

He set her down immediately. "Sorry. I was just trying to help."

It sounded too lame to be the truth. The wariness in her eyes didn't fade and he knew what she was thinking.

Since when did carrying another man's bride across your threshold qualify as help?

Dear Reader,

Welcome back to Collingwood Station, and to Christmas in July. If you've had a chance to read *The Man for Maggie* (June 2007), then you've already met Leslie and Brent—two people who grew up in a small town and have known each other all their lives, yet come from very different backgrounds and have completely different outlooks on life.

I love Christmas. There's something about the spirit of the season that always brings out the best in people, don't you think? I think it would be wonderful to celebrate the holiday more than once a year, so when Leslie decides to host a summer charity event, a Christmas-in-July party seems perfect. Brent has his doubts, but he'll go along with almost anything if it means spending time with Leslie.

It's been fun watching these two overcome their differences while they cope with small-town gossip, a couple of plumbing disasters and the antics of an unruly sheepdog. I hope you enjoy their story. If you have a minute or two, I'd love to have you drop by www.leemckenzie.com for some holiday cheer.

Warmest wishes for a happy holiday,

Lee McKenzie

With This Ring
LEE McKENZIE

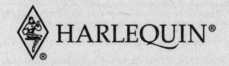

TORONTO • NEW YORK • LONDON
AMSTERDAM • PARIS • SYDNEY • HAMBURG
STOCKHOLM • ATHENS • TOKYO • MILAN • MADRID
PRAGUE • WARSAW • BUDAPEST • AUCKLAND

ISBN-13: 978-0-373-75196-9
ISBN-10:   0-373-75196-6

WITH THIS RING

Printed in U.S.A.

ABOUT THE AUTHOR

From the time she was ten years old and read *Anne of Green Gables* and *Little Women*, Lee McKenzie knew she wanted to be a writer, just like Anne and Jo. In the intervening years she has written everything from advertising copy to an honors thesis in paleontology, but becoming a four-time Golden Heart finalist and a Harlequin author are among her proudest accomplishments. Lee and her artist/teacher husband live on an island along Canada's west coast, and she loves to spend time with two of her best friends—her grown-up children.

Books by Lee McKenzie

HARLEQUIN AMERICAN ROMANCE
1167—THE MAN FOR MAGGIE

To the memory of
Hilda Ilvonen Barrie
and
Meghan Ilvonen McAnally

Chapter One

Brent Borden pulled his flatbed truck onto the quiet, tree-lined street. The road was not a direct route from the lumberyard to the construction site—far from it—and he'd be the first to admit that he'd driven by the church on purpose. According to the clock on the dashboard, the ceremony would start any minute, so he couldn't have said exactly what he was looking for. Closure, maybe. But he sure as hell never expected to see the bride running down the sidewalk.

Barefoot.

In the rain.

Away from the church.

He eased off the accelerator and peered through the blurred windshield. It was Leslie, all right. So he did what anyone would have done. He pulled over, leaned across the cab and wound down the window.

"Need a ride?"

FOR THE first time in her life, Leslie Durrance had no idea where she was going and, furthermore, she didn't care. Anything would be better than what she had just left behind. Except maybe this. She had no intention of accepting help from a free-and-easy construction worker who also happened to be her brother's best friend and, quite possibly, the most annoying man in the world.

"Hey, need a ride?" he asked again.

She slowed her pace but kept moving. "No, thank you."

"Are you lost?"

She hitched the soggy skirt of the satin and lace Armani gown a little higher and shook her head.

"I see." His truck inched along beside her. "Do you know you're going in the wrong direction?"

She stopped then and glared at him through the partly open window. "I know exactly what I'm doing and where I'm going."

He braked. "So you don't need a lift?"

She wanted to say no, but the inside of his truck looked very inviting. Warm and dry, and just about the last place anyone in Collingwood Station would look for her.

As though he sensed her hesitation, he leaned across the cab and opened the door. "Hop in."

What choice did she have? It wouldn't be long before someone came looking for her, and looking for answers.

She hiked up her dress and climbed into the truck.

"Where to?" Brent's voice held a hint of concern but he seemed surprisingly nonplussed by the ridiculousness of the situation.

Where could she go? Not to her town house, or to her mother's house. Those would be the first two places people would look for her. Her office building was closed on Saturdays and she didn't have the keys with her. She was too mortified to go to any of her friends for help. Besides, they were all still inside the church. A hotel? Not without some cash and a credit card.

She had no plan and no place to go, and some crazy twist of fate had landed her in the cab of a truck with a man she'd rejected more times than she could count.

"Why did you stop?" she asked. "After all the things I've

said to you over the years, it wouldn't have surprised me if you'd just driven by."

The wounded look that flickered in his eyes was one she'd seen before. "You really think that little of me?" he asked, running his hand through his dark wavy hair that was, as it always had been, just a tad too long to be manageable.

She lowered her gaze and realized she was still clutching the stupid shoes she'd taken off so she could run faster. "No. Right now, that's how little I think of myself."

He didn't respond to that. Instead, he reached behind the seat and pulled out a jean jacket. "You must be cold. Lean forward a bit."

She was too numb to feel anything, but she couldn't stop shivering, so he was probably right.

He draped the faded denim around her shoulders and she snuggled into it.

The workmanlike scent of sawdust was oddly comforting. "Do you think we could just drive around for a while till I figure out what to do?" This morning she'd thought this New England summer storm might ruin her wedding. Now it was the least of her worries.

"You're soaking wet and you want drive around town with a truckload of lumber?"

No. She wanted to crawl under a rock and die. She turned to face him and his eyes softened immediately.

"How 'bout we go to my place?" he suggested.

Nice try, she thought. "You can't be serious."

"This isn't high school, Leslie. I'm not going to make a pass at you. You can get dried off and warmed up, and take all the time you need to figure out what you want to do. But if you have a better idea—"

She felt like an idiot. He was being very sweet about this, a lot sweeter than she deserved. "Thank you. Your place will be fine."

SLOWLY MANEUVERING the oversized truck through town gave him the opportunity to glance at her from time to time. "You want to talk about what happened?"

"No."

"Okay. I wasn't trying to pry or anything. Just thought you might want to—"

"I don't want to talk about it."

"Got it. I live across town. We'll be there in five minutes or so."

They made the drive in silence, during which he was acutely aware of the change from the stately old residences that surrounded the church to the much smaller and often run-down houses in his neighborhood. The drive also gave him time to ponder this unexpected turn of events. Whatever it was that had made her run, it had to be serious. Leslie Durrance didn't do things like this. For as long as he'd known her, which had been pretty much his whole life, he couldn't ever remember her doing anything impulsive. She'd been on the honor roll and the student council. Then she'd gone to college and law school, just like everyone knew she would. She'd been the prettiest girl in school and he couldn't remember a time when he hadn't been completely crazy about her.

He'd always known the two of them would never work. Why would she settle for him when she could have any guy she set her sights on? She was from a wealthy, prominent family. He'd been raised by his mother in subsidized housing. A quick sideways glance assured him nothing had changed. She wore a necklace and earrings that had more diamonds than he'd ever seen outside a jewelry store. He stole a second look. Her engagement ring must have cost as much as he earned in two years. Maybe more.

He pulled the truck into his driveway, shut off the engine and turned to face her. "Here we are."

She sat motionless, as though she might be having second thoughts. He could hardly blame her.

"Sit tight. I'll come around and get the door for you." If anything, the rain was coming down even harder than when he'd picked her up by the church. He jogged around the front of the truck and by the time he got to her door, his T-shirt was soaking wet. He opened the door and offered her a hand while being careful to keep his distance.

She placed her small, slender hand into his. For once she seemed willing to accept a little help without putting up a fight.

"You're freezing," he said. "Come on. Let's get you inside."

She was still clutching her shoes in her free hand but she managed to gather up the skirt of the wedding gown and step out of the truck. He should probably offer to take the shoes from her, but he sensed she'd only let him do so much before she let him have it.

"Ow!" She stumbled slightly when her bare feet touched the gravel.

Without giving her a chance to protest, he swung her off the ground and headed for the shelter of the veranda. With one arm supporting her shoulders and the other hooked behind her knees, he fumbled with the keys and finally found the lock.

"Brent?"

He looked down into her wide brown eyes and his hand froze on the knob. "What?"

"Put me down," she whispered. "Please." Her voice caught on the last word and came out in a little sob.

He set her down immediately. "Sorry. I was just trying to help."

It sounded too lame to be the truth, even though it was. The wariness in Leslie's eyes didn't fade and he knew what she was thinking.

Smooth move, Borden. Since when did carrying another man's bride across your threshold qualify as helpful?

LESLIE hadn't given any thought to where Brent lived but she never would have predicted an old cottage that had been so carefully restored. She stopped inside the front door and looked around.

He came up behind her and she felt his hand on her back. "Something wrong?"

She shook her head. "What a charming little house."

"You sound surprised." He sounded offended.

"I just meant that it's charming and it's been beautifully restored and—" Hmm. Given that he worked for her brother's construction company, he'd probably done the work himself. Still, the house seemed out of character for the Brent Borden she used to know, which suggested he probably hadn't done this alone. "Did someone help you with it?"

He guided her into the entryway and closed the door. "You think I can't fix up a house without a woman's help?"

This was not going well. "I'm sorry." How many times had she said that since he'd picked her up? "I'm not thinking too clearly. All I wanted to say is that you've done a great job. So, you live here alone?"

"No."

Her brother had mentioned recently that Brent wasn't married, but it made sense that someone as offhandedly charming and, let's face it, downright sexy as Brent would have a woman in his life. Maybe even the one she'd seen him with at Donaldson's Deli, not long after she'd moved back to Connecticut. Her stomach gave an odd little lurch.

"She won't mind you bringing me here?" Stupid question. How many women would be happy to have their partner bring home a fugitive bride?

He eased around her, which brought him even closer. "I guess I could have called and left a message, but I'm pretty much used to doing whatever I want."

More than anything, Leslie wanted to slap the smirk off his

face, but the way he handled his relationship was none of her business. "Some things never change."

He did a mini eye roll. "You got that right. But you're here now so you might as well come in and meet Max."

Max? Unusual name for a woman.

Brent kicked off his boots and walked across the living room and through the kitchen.

Leslie waited by the front door, not sure if she should venture farther until she knew what Max's reaction would be. Besides, her dress was making a puddle on the floor and she didn't want to make an even bigger mess of the gleaming hardwood.

A door opened and closed and that was followed by the sound of skittering on linoleum and by Brent's voice. "Hey, boy, glad to see me? Come on. Yeah, good boy. Come on. Somebody wants to meet you."

Max was a dog. And a boy dog at that. Brent had rescued her from an impossible situation and brought her here until she could figure out what to do next, and she'd insulted him and made herself look even more foolish. What was it about this man that brought out the worst in her?

No, that wasn't fair. That made it sound as though this was his fault, and it wasn't. A better question was, why did she still overreact to everything he said?

Before she could figure out the answer, a huge gray and white sheepdog bounded across the living room, heading straight for her.

"Max! Down!"

Max planted his front paws on the floor and skidded to stop in front of her, his entire back end wagging. He gazed at her through a shaggy curtain of fur.

"Max, sit."

The dog's ears perked up and he glanced back at his master as if checking to see if he really meant what he said.

"Sit."

Max slowly lowered his wagging haunches to the floor.

Leslie patted his head. "Good boy."

Humor sparkled in Brent's eyes. "He doesn't always behave but what he lacks in manners, he makes up for with enthusiasm."

That makes two of you, she thought, but resisted the urge to say it out loud. After the way Brent had rescued her this morning, that would be unfair.

And at least Max hadn't turned out to be the woman she'd seen him with at the deli. She'd seemed a little young for Brent, anyway. They had been sitting at a table that Saturday morning, his arm draped across the back of her chair. They were leaning close and gazing into each other's eyes, and then she'd dipped her finger into the foam of her cappuccino and offered it to him. From the way he looked at her and took her finger into his mouth, it was obvious the two of them had spent the night together.

Brent hadn't seen Leslie, so she'd quickly moved to the counter, her back toward him. After she'd made her purchase and chatted briefly with old Mr. Donaldson, she turned away from the counter and caught Brent watching her. His smile had been a combination of surprise and his old good-natured, happy-to-see-you charm. She'd given him a brief nod in return and hurried out of the shop. In high school she'd had to spend a certain amount of time with him because he was her brother's best friend. This was no longer high school, and she was glad to see that he'd found someone to be with.

Half an hour later she'd finished shopping and was loading her purchases into the trunk of her car when she saw Brent helping Cappuccino Girl into his old blue and white truck. His hand had curled over her butt and lingered just a little too long.

Leslie withdrew her hand from the coarse, wiry fur on Max's head and pulled the denim jacket more snugly around her shoulders as she shivered.

"You must be freezing," Brent said. "Let's get you warmed up."

She glanced at him warily.

He rolled his eyes again but didn't comment on her reaction. "Maybe a hot bath while I see if I can find some dry clothes that will fit you?"

"A hot bath would be wonderful." She set her shoes on the floor and was again aware of the puddle that her dripping dress had made. "Look at this mess. I'm so sorry."

"It's just water," Brent said. "I'll wipe it up, if Max doesn't get to it first. The bathroom's through here."

Max leaped to his feet and trotted next to him, through an archway that led to a small space that couldn't really be called a hallway, since it was only as long as it was wide.

Leslie followed, noticing for the first time just how tall and broad shouldered Brent was.

Most of the tiny bathroom was taken up by the biggest claw-foot tub she'd ever seen. She could hardly wait to get out of the cold, wet dress and into a tubful of hot water.

"There's a shower if you'd prefer that." He indicated the curtain suspended from a brass rail over the tub.

She shook her head.

Without a word, he inserted a plug in the drain and turned on the taps.

Max settled himself on the bath mat.

"Help yourself to towels," Brent said, pointing to a wall shelf, "and anything else you need. I'll see what I can find for you to wear."

"Thank you." She hoped he meant something of his because she would die of embarrassment if he produced another woman's clothing.

Once he was out of the room, she slipped his jacket off her shoulders and hung it on a hook on the back of the door. The cool air raised goose bumps on her arms and shoulders.

Shivering almost uncontrollably, she stretched one arm over her shoulder to unzip the back of her dress. It was just out of reach. She extended her other arm around her back and still couldn't unfasten it. Getting into the thing hadn't been a problem because Allison and Candice, her brides-maids, had been there to help. At least, Allison had helped. Candice, not so much.

An inviting cloud of steam rose from the water in the tub. Maybe she should just climb in, dress and all. Or find a pair of scissors and cut her way out of the damn thing. The very idea sent a giggle rising up her throat. Not even in her current state could she destroy such a beautiful and expensive gown.

Max's dark, soulful eyes stared up at her.

"Whatever you do, don't ever get married."

"Excuse me?" Brent stood in the doorway.

"Sorry. I was talking to Max."

"Ah, I see. I don't think there's much danger of him doing anything rash. He and I have already had that talk, and besides…" Brent shielded his mouth with one hand and spoke in an exaggerated whisper. "He's been fixed."

She refused to let herself be baited again. "You'll have to give me the name of his surgeon. I know someone who would benefit from that procedure."

"Ouch. I'll have to be careful to stay on your good side."

"Good plan."

"All right, then." He handed her a pair of gray sweatpants, a long-sleeved blue T-shirt and a thick pair of black cotton socks. "This is the best I can do. The pants have a draw-string," he said, glancing at her waist. He stepped closer and she quickly backed away, narrowly missing Max's paw.

Brent leaned over the tub and turned off the taps.

"I can look after that," she said.

His sharp glance had her wishing, yet again, that she

could stop overreacting. "I'm sorry. I appreciate everything you're doing."

"No trouble. While you're in the bath, I'll run out and pick up some more clothes for you."

"You don't have to do that. I can—" She paused. She could do what? Go back to her town house and deal with Gerald and her mother? No way. "Thank you. But please keep the receipts and I'll pay you back."

He gave her an odd look. "I wasn't planning to go shopping. My mother collects clothing for the homeless shelter, so she always has things on hand. Everything will be secondhand, but it'll be clean and mended."

"Oh."

"Unless that's not going to work for you."

What he meant was, unless that's not *good enough* for you. She could hardly blame him for having such a low opinion of her.

She squared her shoulders and wished she could stop shivering. "Since I'm temporarily homeless, that'll work just fine. Please thank your mother for me. When my life gets backs to normal, I'll have the clothes dry-cleaned and return them." Under the circumstances, it was the least she could do.

"I'll be sure to tell her." He looked as though he'd like to say more. Whatever it was, she was glad he kept it to himself. She was on the verge of tears again, and the last thing she wanted was for him to try to console her.

He fished his keys from his pocket, and Max jumped up right away. "Sorry, boy, not this time. You stay here with Leslie."

The dog's tail-wagging—assuming there was a tail under all that fur—subsided only slightly as he looked from Brent to her and back again.

"You can take him with you. I'll be fine."

"I'm sure you will be. Still, I'll leave him here. He'll let you know if anyone comes to the door and he'll keep barking until they leave. You won't have to bother answering, and you'll know when they're gone."

"Are you expecting someone?" Since she was absolutely certain that no one would come here looking for her, she could only assume that Brent didn't want any of his potential visitors to know she was here.

"No one in particular. Your brother's been known to show up, though, and I just thought that given what's happened…"

Of course. That possibility hadn't occurred to her. "Good thinking. I don't want to see anyone right now." Especially not her family.

"I don't get a lot of company, so it looks like you've come to the right place."

She looked longingly at the steam rising from the tub. "Thanks again," she said, clenching her jaw to keep her teeth from chattering. "I really do appreciate this."

"You're freezing. I'll get out of your way." He was out the door before she remembered the zipper.

"Brent?"

He looked back. "Yeah?"

She turned sideways and pointed over her shoulder. "Um…I can't reach the zipper. Would you mind?"

He looked as though he'd rather wrestle a grizzly bear, but he slowly stepped back into the room. "Turn around," he said gruffly.

She complied and stood stock-still. The day had been filled with unexpected situations. What was one more?

Firm fingers brushed her skin. She closed her eyes, as if that might somehow block out his touch. No such luck.

The length of time it took him to undo the hook-and-eye closure at the top of the zipper was proof that the tiny device had not been designed for big workman's hands. When it finally gave way, his breath came out in a rush, as if he'd been holding it, and sent a delicious shower of warm air down the back of her neck.

The zipper gave him no trouble at all and when it neared her waist, he let go all of a sudden and backed away. "You can manage the rest." And then he was gone.

Startled, Leslie opened her eyes.

The front door opened and banged shut.

Max's ears perked up and he dashed out of the room.

For a few seconds she'd actually forgotten where she was, and who was undressing her. No, that wasn't the truth. Every heightened nerve ending and every inch of chilled skin had been perfectly well aware of who was doing the undressing. *Careful,* she warned herself. *That's one place you never wanted to go, and now is not the time to consider it.*

She had every intention of having a quick bath and being dressed by the time Brent returned, but just to be safe she closed the bathroom door and turned the lock.

She shimmied out of the dress and let it fall to the floor. The air against her damp skin made her shiver. She quickly unfastened her wet bra and dropped it onto the dress. She tried to slide her panties down her legs. The damp fabric stuck to her thighs but she finally managed to roll them off.

She stepped into the bath and lowered herself into the water, gasping slightly as her cold skin adjusted to the warmth. Then she rested her head against the back of the tub and closed her eyes. The dangling, diamond-studded strands of her earrings grazed her shoulders. She slipped them off and reached for the clasp of the necklace. The jewelry had been a wedding gift from Gerald. She reached over the edge of the tub and tossed them onto the dress.

She slid deeper into the tub, hot water swooshing around her shoulders. She wanted to be furious with Gerald, but she was having trouble mustering any real anger. Loathing. Disgust. Definitely those. As the wedding date had drawn closer, she'd started to feel antsy and unsure of herself. She didn't believe in premonitions, but maybe her subconscious had been picking up things that she hadn't wanted—or even been ready—to acknowledge.

Things like what a two-timing, no-good son of a bitch she'd almost married. Luckily she'd found out about his affair *before* the ceremony and not afterward.

She was even grateful for the bizarre twist of fate that had landed her here. Brent's timely rescue had bought her some precious time. No one knew where she was, and when she finally did see her family and her good-for-nothing slimeball of an ex-fiancé, it would be on her terms.

By now Gerald would have figured out that she'd seen him with another woman. And not just any woman, but one of her bridesmaids, one of her best friends. Meanwhile he'd be trying to convince everyone that today's disastrous events had been her fault.

She squeezed her eyes shut in an attempt to block out the image of the two of them in the back of the coat room at the church.

A big, fat tear rolled down her cheek. You will not cry, she told herself. Gerald Bedford III and Candice Bentley-Ferguson deserved each other. Not only were they cut from the same bolt, they'd each chosen someone who was bound to cheat on them.

Leslie opened her eyes and reached for a bar of soap. The ring on her left hand sparkled.

Damn it.

It was a gorgeous ring. She'd been the envy of everyone she knew, and probably lots she didn't. When Gerald had given it to her, it had represented everything that was right about their relationship. They were young successful professionals with brilliant futures. They had everything going for them.

Why wasn't that enough? Better question. Why wasn't she good enough for him?

In spite of her best efforts to hold the tears at bay, her eyes filled up and the room blurred. Today she was supposed to cross number five off her Life List. She slid the ring off her finger and tossed it into the soap dish. She'd earned the right to a little self-pity, as long as she got herself under control before Brent came home with her hand-me-downs.

BRENT SLAMMED the gear shift into Reverse and backed out of the driveway as fast as a ton of lumber would allow. Leslie probably thought he was a lunatic for tearing out on her like that, but he'd had a hard-on that would stop a train and there had only been two possible outcomes.

Either he'd do something he'd regret, or he'd get the hell out of there *before* he did something he'd regret.

The feel of her skin, the scent of her damp, sweet-smelling hair and the sight of her lacy white bra were now branded into his brain, and still had his libido on full alert. Which might account for his uncharacteristically bad driving, although it would make a lousy defense if he crashed into someone. He eased off the accelerator and brought the truck to a stop at a red light, chiding himself for being such an idiot.

She'd always made it abundantly and sometimes scathingly clear she didn't want to have anything to do with him. In the seventh grade, at Candice Bentley's birthday party, he'd finagled his way into playing seven minutes in heaven with her. That kiss had lasted somewhere in the neighborhood of four seconds.

Leslie had been a little slip of a girl in those days but she'd packed a mighty wallop.

Undaunted, he'd pursued her through high school. It had actually turned into a game, and he'd always been the loser.

He would ask her out. She'd say no.

He'd call her. She'd hang up.

He'd tuck a note into her locker. She'd scrunch it into a ball and toss it in the trash.

A horn honking behind him told him the light had turned green. He was glad to have an excuse to get away from her for a while. Too bad it meant going to his mother's place though. She would question his sudden need for women's clothing, and he'd never been any good at flying under her radar.

Maybe she wouldn't be home, he thought. He could just help himself to whatever he could find and she'd be none the wiser. He pulled up along the curb and spotted her ancient Dodge station wagon in the driveway. No such luck.

He sprinted through the rain to the back door and let himself in. "Mom? You home?"

"In here, dear. What brings you by this morning?"

He followed his nose into the kitchen. She was making chicken stew. "It's almost lunchtime. And since when do I need a reason to visit the most gorgeous woman in Collingwood Station?"

"Since you're blocking the street with a truckload of building materials and trying to use that sweet talk on someone who knows better than to fall for it."

"We were supposed to start a new job on Monday. I have to deliver that load to the site sometime today, so I won't be here for long." He crossed the kitchen and planted a kiss on the top of her head.

"What do you mean by 'supposed to'?" she asked.

"I might be tied up with something else for a few days." He reached over her shoulder and snagged a piece of raw carrot from the pile on the chopping block.

"Watch it, young man, or you might lose one of those fingers."

He laughed. "I'll take my chances. Are you expecting company?" he asked. If the size of the stewpot was anything to go by, she was cooking for a crowd.

"I thought I'd make enough for a meal or two for myself and take the rest to the shelter. They're a little short on food this weekend."

At this rate she'd never be able to retire, but talking to her about it was a losing battle. She'd carry the weight of the whole world on her shoulders if anyone asked her to. His mother was younger than most of the mothers of his friends, but she often looked tired and older than she actually was. Today was one of those days.

She'd become a single parent at sixteen and had struggled through a lot of hardship. He remembered her helping him with homework while she studied and worked to put herself through college. Nothing had changed when she became a social worker. In spite of an ample salary, she still lived in the little old house she'd purchased twenty years ago, and somehow she managed to keep her geriatric Dodge running. Every spare penny went to help those who were less fortunate than she was.

She tossed handfuls of diced carrots and celery into the pot and started on the potatoes. "So, you haven't told me what brings you by."

He might as well cut to the chase. "I need to borrow a few things."

"What would you like? And don't tell me it's take-out chicken stew. If you want any of that, you'll have to come back and have dinner with me."

"Sorry. No can do."

"Your loss." She gave him one of her big, warm smiles. "So if it's not food, what *are* you after?"

"I need some women's clothing. Enough for a few days. Size four," he said. "If you have anything."

She set her knife on the butcher block and wiped her hands on a towel as she turned to face him.

"That's an odd request."

"Not really. A friend of mine is in kind of a jam and she needs a few things. Just temporarily, until…"

His explanation trailed off as his mother's scrutiny intensified.

"Please tell me this friend of yours isn't Leslie Durrance."

Damn, she was good.

Chapter Two

"Why would you ask that?" As soon as he said it, he knew his evasiveness sounded like a yes.

And his mother's eagle eye never missed a trick. "I stopped by Donaldson's Deli to pick up the day-old bread that Mr. Donaldson donates to the shelter. The place was buzzing. Apparently she bolted and left Gerald whatshis-name at the altar."

"Man, what is it with this town and gossip?"

"You haven't answered my question, and that usually means—"

"Okay, fine. She's at my place," he confessed. Yes, at that very moment Leslie Durrance was in his bathtub. Naked and single. "And she has nothing to wear but a soaking-wet wedding dress and a pair of high-heeled shoes."

"Do I even dare ask how she ended up with you?"

"I was driving by the church—"

"Oh, Brent. You can't be serious."

"What do you mean?"

"You might be able to fool yourself, but you can't fool me. I thought you were over her years ago but even if you're not, why torture yourself by driving by the church on her wedding day?"

He hated it when she looked at him like he was one of her homeless people. He didn't want her to be concerned about him. He should be taking care of her for a change. "Under the circumstances it's a good thing I showed up when I did."

"Because?"

"She needed help."

His mother let out a long sigh. "She's a millionaire, Brent. She can buy anything she wants, when she wants it, without asking how much it costs. Why would she need your help?"

The sparkle of that enormous diamond ring flashed in his memory. "Well, she didn't have her purse with her."

His mother burst out laughing. "You dear, sweet boy. I guess I shouldn't be surprised that my Prince Charming would race to her rescue."

"It's not like that, Mom. She hasn't told me what happened, but I know Leslie. She wouldn't run out on her wedding unless something really bad had happened. I get the feeling she wants to lie low for a couple of days and there's no way she can do that in Collingwood Station, money or no money, without a little help from someone."

She rested her hand against the side of his face. "And that someone had to be you. At the very least, I hope she appreciates this. And who knows, maybe she'll come to her senses and realize she couldn't possibly do any better."

Yeah, that should happen right around the time money started to grow on trees. He covered her hand with his. "I wouldn't count on that. Besides, like I said, that's not what this is about. She's in a tight spot and I was there to help."

"Still, I can't help wondering if your timing was good or bad."

When he didn't respond, she sighed again. "There's always a first time for everything and this is definitely the first time I've had to provide clothing for a homeless millionaire, but you're in luck. I just finished cleaning and mending all the clothes that were donated this month. I was going to take them into the shelter on Monday."

"She said she'll have everything cleaned and return it."

"How generous."

"Come on, Mom. It's not her fault that people are homeless."

"Whose fault is it?"

Here we go, he thought. Once she climbed on her soapbox, he knew better than to argue. "If I ask, I'm sure she'll make a donation, too."

"Too bad you have to ask."

All righty then. "She's not a bad person, Mom."

"She is if she breaks your heart again." She turned back to her food preparation. "The clothes are on the bed in your old room. I sorted them into piles by size, so you shouldn't have any trouble finding something that'll fit her."

"Thanks. I really appreciate this. So does Leslie."

He didn't get a response, so he headed up the stairs.

This old house held a lot of memories. Good ones. The door to his old room creaked when he opened it. He'd been on his own for a lot of years so it surprised him that his mother had never reclaimed this space. His baseball trophies were still lined up on the dresser and an old Reggie Jackson poster was tacked to the closet door.

The clothing for the homeless shelter had been carefully arranged in piles on the bed. He picked through the small-sized women's clothing and chose a pair of jeans that looked as though they should fit her, a pair of faded yellow shorts and a couple of T-shirts. The pink one looked great, actually. In high school she'd had an undetermined number of sweaters in every shade of pink imaginable, and every single one of them had suited her perfectly. He hadn't thought of it in years but if anyone had a signature color, Leslie did. And it was pink.

He'd never forgotten how beautiful she'd looked the night of his senior prom. Had she been wearing pink that night? Probably. Technically it hadn't been her prom, since she'd been in her junior year, but she was on the student council, which apparently meant she was on the prom committee, too. He'd asked her to be his date and of course she'd said no, so he'd gone solo in a futile attempt to prove a point. Undaunted, he'd waited and watched until finally, near the end of the night, she'd been sitting alone at her table and the band was playing a slow song. He'd asked her to dance and in a moment of apparent weakness, she'd accepted.

Aside from that stolen adolescent kiss in her friend's closet, that dance had been the only other time he'd ever touched her, and he'd never forgotten it. That time their kiss had lasted significantly longer and had been a whole lot sweeter. The instant the song ended she'd pulled herself away and marched off the dance floor, but at least that time she hadn't slugged him.

He gave his head a shake in an attempt to dispel the memories and surveyed the rest of the clothing piled on the bed. There was an assortment of undergarments, which he quickly ruled out as being way too personal, but he added a nightgown to the things he'd already chosen. He unfolded a sleeveless red dress that looked like something a hooker might wear and quickly put it back.

After bundling the clothes under his arm, he took one last look around. A pile of stuffed animals on the desk caught his eye. They must be for the shelter, too, because he didn't recognize any of them. He picked up a toy dog and put it down, then examined a small brown teddy bear.

Maybe this wasn't such a good idea. The clothes he'd chosen were the best he could find, but they weren't good enough for Leslie. Not because she was a millionaire, but because she was special. She deserved the best. Like his mother did.

He closed the door and clattered down the narrow staircase.

"Find what you need?" his mother asked, apparently back to her usual good-natured self.

The mouthwatering aroma of his favorite dinner filled the room. "Yeah, thanks. This should be fine." He hoped.

His mother gave the pot a stir, then set her wooden spoon on a spoon rest next to the stove. "Let me find a bag for those things."

She returned from the back porch with a canvas shopping bag and held it open for him. Her eyebrows arched into a silent question when she spied the bear.

He responded with a silent challenge of his own.

"Those toys are for the shelter, too. We do get children from time to time."

"I thought it might make her feel better." No, that wasn't true. He had no idea how she would react to it, but he'd feel better if it distracted her attention from the shabby clothing he'd found for her. He handed the toy to his mother. "Sorry. I wasn't thinking."

She set the bear on the kitchen table. "Does she need shoes?"

He dumped the clothes into the bag and tucked it under his arm. Geez, he hadn't thought about shoes, but of course she needed some. Those crazy high heels she'd been carrying were completely impractical. "What have you got?"

"Not much. Do you know what size?"

He shook his head.

"I bought myself some new sandals the other day and haven't worn them yet. Take those and see if they fit."

"Mom, you don't have to—"

"I have other shoes, and I'm sure she'll replace them."

"I'm sure she will. Thanks."

"What about toiletries?"

"What?"

"Toothbrush, deodorant, moisturizer, makeup." Mischief glimmered in her eyes. "Feminine hygiene."

He felt his face go red. "Geez, I don't know. She never said anything about that kind of stuff."

She laughed. "If you really want to be a hero, you should make a stop at the drugstore on your way home."

He stared at her. Was she serious?

"At least buy her a toothbrush."

FREDERICK'S PHARMACY seemed unusually busy. He wandered up one aisle and down the next, trying to figure out what Leslie might need. In the end he settled on a toothbrush—a bright pink one that would not get confused with his blue one—and headed for the checkout.

The guy in line ahead of him glanced over his shoulder and nodded.

John Fontaine. Allison Fontaine's husband. Allison would have been a maid of honor today, if there had been a wedding. Judging by John's boutonniered tuxedo, he'd been in the wedding party, too.

Brent nodded back. "How's it going?"

"I've had better days."

"Is that right?" It sounded lame, but he couldn't think of anything else to say.

"You can probably tell I'm supposed to be at a wedding reception right now," he said, as if trying to explain the monkey suit.

"I kind of figured. Who's getting married?"

"A friend of mine. Gerald Bedford. Maybe you know him?"

Brent had always known Leslie would never settle for a guy like him, but when he'd heard that she planned to marry Gerald Bedford III, it had been like a knife in the gut. "I know who he is. Who's he marrying?"

John looked confused. "Leslie Durrance. I assumed you'd know. You still work for her brother, Nick, don't you?"

"Oh, right," he said. "I think he mentioned something about a wedding."

"I might as well tell you, since you'll hear about it from

Nick anyway. There was no wedding because Leslie took off. Literally left the groom standing at the altar."

"You're kidding." Brent opened his eyes wide and hoped that passed for surprise. "You don't hear about that happening very often, except maybe in the movies."

"It was quite a scene."

"I can imagine. What happened? She get cold feet or something?"

John gave an expansive shrug. "She just took off. No one seems to know why, and no one knows where she went."

"Humph. Go figure." Did anyone think to ask the groom what he'd done to her? Brent wished he could think of a way to fish for more information without raising suspicion. On the other hand, much as he'd like to know what the hell Gerald Bedford had done to hurt Leslie, he'd rather hear her side of the story first.

"Nick's out looking for her, and her mother's not handling it very well."

The cashier started ringing up John's purchases—an assortment of things that could only be described as toiletries, right down to the dreaded box of "feminine hygiene." John folded his list and stuck it in his pocket. "Picking up a few things for my wife. She's pretty upset, not knowing where Leslie is."

"Understandable." He should have had the sense to ask Leslie if she needed anything besides clothes. Still, he was just as happy to not be standing here with a basketful of women's toiletries. He tossed the pink toothbrush on the counter, then met John's questioning gaze. "I have to clean the grout in the bathroom," he said.

"That'll be eighteen dollars and ninety-seven cents," the cashier said.

John opened his wallet and handed her a hundred-dollar bill.

"Yep," Brent said. "Toothbrushes are great on grout."

"I'll remember that." John pocketed his wallet and picked up the bag. "Guess I'll see you around."

"You bet."

John started to walk away, then stopped. "You know, most guys wouldn't be telling people they were buying a spare toothbrush to clean grout."

Brent pulled a couple of loose bills out of his pocket and smiled. Guess I'm not your average guy, he thought to himself as he watched John cross the parking lot.

"Will that be everything?" the cashier asked.

"No, I'll take one of these, too." From a bin near the checkout he chose a small brown teddy bear with a pink ribbon tied around its neck and placed it on the counter beside the toothbrush.

LESLIE STEPPED out of the bath, feeling a little calmer and a lot warmer, and toweled herself dry. She picked up her bra and panties and dropped them again. After that wonderful warm bath, there was no way she could wear cold, wet underwear. She pulled Brent's T-shirt over her head, breathing in the clean, fresh-but-still-masculine scent, and reached for his sweat pants.

She'd never worn a man's clothing before and the whisper of the fleecy fabric was unexpectedly intimate, especially against the part of her that should have been wearing underwear. After she adjusted the drawstring and tied it, the pants settled comfortably onto her hips. The legs were way too long so she rolled them up, then slipped her feet into the socks.

Her beautiful wedding gown was a crumpled heap on the floor. She set the jewelry on the edge of the vanity and shook out the dress over the tub. It was an absolute dream of a dress. Or at least it had been until she'd run through the rain in it. It had been the first and only dress she'd tried on and even Allison, who never bought anything until she'd tried on half the things in the store, had agreed it was perfect.

Everything about this day was supposed to be perfect. But she had been so preoccupied with planning the perfect wedding that she'd missed seeing that the perfect groom was cheating on her.

She hung the dress on a hook on the back of the bathroom door, next to Brent's jacket. After she'd neatly draped her wet towels over the towel bar, she gathered up her bra and panties. "Brent, I really hope you have a clothes dryer here."

She opened the bathroom door and Max, who must have been sprawled on the floor outside, leaped to his feet.

"Were you guarding the door?"

His tail wagged in response.

"Good boy. Is Brent home yet?"

The dog cocked his head to one side.

"I take it that means no." Besides, the house was small enough that she would have heard him come in. "Is it okay if I have a look around?"

The tiny hallway was lined with doors. Aside from the bathroom, there were two closets and two bedrooms. Both bedroom doors were open. The one with the huge four-poster bed and chest of drawers must be Brent's. The other had a desk, a small bookcase crammed with books and magazines, and a neatly made single bed. Until now she hadn't given any thought to where she might spend the night, but found herself hoping it would be here. Too bad there was no way to let Gerald know she'd be spending the night with another man.

Except Brent hadn't offered to keep her overnight.

And even if he did, she wouldn't technically be spending the night *with* him. But then Gerald wouldn't need to know that.

Max disappeared into Brent's bedroom, but she decided not to follow. Instead she went through to the living room.

Max loped into the room behind her, carrying a gray teddy bear in his mouth.

"How adorable are you? Is that your favorite toy?"

He set the bear on the floor between them.

"Are you giving it to me?"

He wagged his back end.

She reached for the bear but he grabbed it and dashed out of reach.

"So that's how it's going to be." She clapped her hands and Max trotted ahead of her into the kitchen. Leslie followed. No doubt he expected her to chase him, but first she had to dry her underwear and there was no laundry equipment in here.

Surely he had a washer and dryer? She returned to the hallway by the bathroom and opened a pair of folding doors. Sure enough, there was a washer and dryer. She took a quick look at the care tag sewn into her bra. It wasn't supposed to go in the dryer but desperate times…

"As if ruined lingerie is the worst thing that could happen today." She tossed both garments into the dryer and closed the door. Five minutes on low should do it, she decided. With any luck she'd be wearing them by the time Brent returned.

She went back to the kitchen. She loved well-equipped kitchens, and Brent had done an amazing job of fixing up this one. It even had an old wood-burning cookstove that appeared to have been converted to gas. She was impressed.

Max dropped his bear on the floor next to an empty bowl and gazed up at her. As if she wasn't already falling for the silly mutt, his pleading look was completely irresistible.

"Your dish is empty. Would you like something to eat?"

His tongue rolled out the side of his mouth.

"Poor Max. Where does Brent keep your food?"

She looked at him for a moment, then shook her head. "It's one thing to talk to a dog. Waiting for an answer is a good indication that you're losing your mind."

She opened the fridge. Three bottles of beer, an empty pizza box and an assortment of individual-sized condiments.

In spite of the impressive kitchen, it appeared that Brent ate out a lot. And there was no dog food. She opened the cupboard nearest the dog's empty dish.

Max leaped to his feet, nearly knocking her over in the process, and raced back and forth across the kitchen.

Inside the cupboard was an enormous bag of doggie kibble. She peered into the bag and saw a red plastic scoop. "How much am I supposed to give you?"

For heaven's sake, Leslie, stop asking him questions. She hauled the bag out of the cupboard and read the daily portions, which were broken down by weight.

How much did Max weigh?

At least this time she hadn't asked him. She dumped a scoopful of food into the bowl and Max dove into it eagerly. "That should do for now. If you're supposed to get more, Brent can give it to you when he gets home."

But now that Max had something to eat, he couldn't be less interested in her.

The dryer buzzed. Dry underwear! She hurried back to the hallway, pulled the two items out of the dryer, took them into the bathroom and locked the door. She shed Brent's clothes as quickly as she could and put on her bra and panties. Who knew warm underwear felt this good? She'd have to do this more often. She pulled the shirt and sweat pants back on and tightened the drawstring on her way back to the kitchen.

The ring of the telephone startled her. She had no intention of answering but instinctively she glanced at the call display.

C. Girling.

Cappuccino Girl?

No. They'd gone to high school with someone named Cathy Girling, but she was not the woman who'd been with Brent that day at the deli. However, Cathy *had* been one of the glamour girls in the gaggle of admirers that had followed him around the school. Was Brent seeing her? She'd never seemed like his type.

Not that it's any of your business.

A red light on the phone started to blink. Whoever she was, she'd left a message.

Leslie hefted the dog food bag back into the cupboard and glanced again at the phone. She should call someone and let them know where she was, or at least that she was all right, and she should definitely check her own messages.

She picked up the phone and called Nick. Luckily she reached his answering machine and not him. She left a longer-than-necessary message, telling him she was okay but not where she was or what had happened. They'd drifted apart since they were teenagers and she regretted that. Great as it was that they'd reconnected in the past few weeks, she wasn't ready to hear what he had to say about this disaster.

After she hung up, she called her voice mail to check her messages. There was one from Nick. "Call me," was all he said. Three were from a frantic-sounding Allison, who had already sent her husband to check Leslie's town house and the law office where she worked. There was one from her mother, sternly demanding that she return her call immediately, and two of the calls had been hang-ups. Gerald? He wouldn't call, would he? But trust him not to have the guts to leave a message if he did.

She hung up and looked around the kitchen again. It was neat and tidy, except for a few dishes in the sink. There was no dishwasher and without giving much thought to what she was doing, she filled the sink with hot, soapy water.

The tag on Max's collar jangled loudly against the metal bowl as he wolfed down his lunch. "Must be good stuff, Max," she said.

"You didn't have to wash those."

She dropped the pot she was scrubbing, splashing herself with soapy water as she whirled around. "I didn't hear you come in."

"Sorry. I didn't mean to startle you." Brent had a wide smile but his eyebrows suggested he was a little puzzled. He pointed to Max. "He swindled you into feeding him, did he?"

"His bowl was empty and he seemed hungry, so I thought I'd feed him for you."

The dog looked up from his once-again-empty bowl and licked his chops.

Brent ruffled the fur on the top of his head. "Max, you old rascal."

Leslie dried her hands on a dish towel. "I wasn't supposed to feed him?"

"He only gets fed once a day. I put his food out in the evening."

"I'm so sorry. Will he be all right?"

Brent laughed. "He'll be fine, except now he likes you better than me."

Max was clearly devoted to Brent, but she still liked the idea. "He's a great dog. How old is he?"

"The vet thinks he's about three."

"You haven't had him since he was a puppy?"

He gave the dog an affectionate scruff on the neck. "I found Max at the SPCA. I did some work there last summer, repairing their kennels, and there he was. He had been badly neglected by his previous owner. He needed a home and he seemed to think I needed a dog."

"Poor fellow." She knelt beside him and put an arm around his neck. He licked her ear, making her laugh. "How could anyone not love you?"

"I hear that a lot," Brent said.

"Very funny. I was talking about Max." She stood up and hung the dish towel on a rack near the sink.

Brent looked at her and for a moment he seemed as uncomfortable as she felt. Now that they'd exhausted Max's history, he didn't seem to know what else to say.

"You have a message," she said. "Someone called while you were out."

He picked up the phone and checked the number of the last caller, then gave her a quick, questioning glance.

"I didn't answer it."

"I see that." But he didn't seem to be in any hurry to check it. Instead he handed her the bag he was carrying. "Here's the stuff I found at my mother's place. I'm sorry they're not nicer or…" His voice trailed off.

"I'm sure these things will be fine."

"I bought you a toothbrush."

"Oh. Thank you."

"It was my mother's idea."

Panic grabbed her heart and held on. Brent's mother didn't like her, although she'd never understood why. "You told her I'm here?"

"Didn't have to. She guessed it was you."

"How…?" But she knew how. Collingwood Station had an efficient gossip mill, to which she herself had contributed on more than one occasion. "The news really spread that fast?"

"Afraid so. She went to Donaldson's earlier today and people were talking about it. I ran into John at the drugstore and…"

Oh, no. "Was Allison with him?" When it came to sniffing out gossip and dragging it out of people, Allison had a nose like a bloodhound and a mean streak like a pit bull.

"Apparently she was already at home nursing a headache," he said. "John didn't seem to know why you were gone, but he did mention that Nick was looking for you."

"While you were out I called my brother and left a message on his machine. I didn't tell him where I am, so thank you for covering for me."

"No problem."

She tightened her grip on the bag of clothes as if it was a security blanket, which in a way it was. The things Brent had brought for her meant she wouldn't have to go home for a few days. If he didn't want her to stay here, maybe he'd lend her some money so she could stay at a hotel. "Did your mother know what happened? Why I—"

Brent shook his head. "And my mother's not one to gossip. She won't tell anyone where you're staying."

Leslie supposed she should be relieved to hear that, but she knew Brent's mother. They had served on Collingwood Station's redevelopment committee and from the start, Colleen Borden had treated her like an adversary. Still, she hoped Brent was right and that his mother wouldn't tell anyone she was here.

She wasn't ready to face her family and friends, and she definitely wasn't ready to tell them what had happened. But what about Brent? Did she owe him an explanation?

"Gerald is having an affair," she said, even before she'd made a conscious decision to tell him.

He looked as though he didn't believe her. "Are you sure? I mean, maybe—"

"I saw them together." The flash of memory was accompanied by a wave of nausea.

"Why didn't you dump him when you found out?" He sounded incredulous.

"I found out this morning."

She watched as he processed that piece of information, and then the understanding of what she'd just told him spread across his face.

"You mean he…? They…? At the church? No."

She glanced down at her feet and wriggled her toes inside Brent's socks. "I'm afraid so."

"Oh, Leslie. I'm so sorry." He pulled her into his arms then, and she let him. He felt safe and dependable and surprisingly nonjudgmental, and she pressed her face against his shoulder and let the tears flow. Oddly enough, she wasn't sure what was making her cry—Gerald's infidelity, or having to tell Brent about it.

Chapter Three

Taking her into his arms had been purely instinctive. Reacting to her now that she was in them was perfectly natural, he told himself. Strictly physical. Totally unbelievable. When he'd picked her up by the church, the delicate scent of her perfume had filled the cab of the truck. Now, after using his soap and shampoo, she smelled like she belonged here.

He'd driven by the church that morning with the intention of finally closing a door on one chapter of his life. Instead the door was wide open and the pages of that chapter were blowing all over the room. Which was a really dumb metaphor to be thinking about, considering that the woman of his dreams, the one to which he still compared all others, was now soaking his shirt with her tears. As far he knew she had never in her life needed anyone or anything, but she needed someone now. Not him, specifically, but he was here and she was here, and the bag of clothes he'd given her was squished between them, and that was a good thing.

This isn't about you, he told himself. *Ha. The hell it isn't.*

Meanwhile, he had no clue what to say to her. *There, there, everything will be okay.*

No.

"I'd like to track that guy down and beat the crap out of him."

Or he could say that.

She took half a step back and looked at him through watery eyes. "That sounds like something a brother might say." For the first time that day, she smiled, just briefly, but long enough to remind him about the adorable little dimple to the left of her mouth.

And he was so glad he wasn't her brother. "If yours never said it, he should have."

"Nick never gives advice."

"This time he should have made an exception."

"And what should he have said?"

"Don't marry that guy, he's a jerk."

"He told you that?"

Brent knew thin ice when he was standing on it, and this ice was getting thinner by the minute. "Not in so many words, but he obviously didn't like Gerald."

"He never said anything like that to me."

"He has some misguided idea that he shouldn't stick his nose in other people's business."

"I know. Nick hates having people tell him what to do, so he'd never interfere with anyone else's decision." She looked down at her hands and fidgeted with the handles of the bag of clothing. "So you think Gerald's a jerk and you'd like to beat the crap out of him," she said. "Anything else you want to tell me while we're on the subject?"

The question caught him off guard. *Thin ice,* he reminded himself. "Gerald and I don't exactly move in the same circles so I don't know him all that well."

"But you have an opinion."

And as much as he found it difficult to believe, she seemed to want to hear it. So he said it. "I don't think he's good enough for you."

"Really?"

"That surprises you?"

"A little."

"What did you expect me to say?"

"That we deserved each other."

"Then you don't know me very well."

"You're right. I don't know you at all. You've changed a lot since high school."

He shrugged. "I'm still the same person."

"I guess I didn't know you then, either."

"You never gave me a chance."

"You were always goofing around and trying to get me to go out with you. Now you seem…"

He waited for her to finish her sentence, but she didn't. "Grown-up?" he asked.

There was that dimple again, and he had to resist the urge to stroke the tip of his finger across it.

"Definitely grown-up. And thank you for not…" She stopped herself and her face flushed pink.

I'll be damned, he thought. Had she actually thought he might make a pass at her? He searched those soft brown eyes, looking for a hint of wishful thinking, but detected none.

He moved closer and she stepped back until she was against the kitchen counter. "This is what you expected?" He put his hands on the counter on either side of her and leaned closer but without touching her.

Her eyes went wide.

"This was the last thing on my mind. Under the circumstances, making a pass at you would have been out of line. But now that you've suggested it…"

She eyed him warily. "I didn't suggest anything."

That's right, he reminded himself. If anyone was guilty of wishful thinking, he was.

"I'll just say one more thing," he said as he backed away from her.

"What's that?" Her voice was barely audible.

"I always thought Gerald Bedford was a jerk but until today I never had him pegged as a fool."

"I don't think he is."

"Trust me, he is. And when he realizes how badly he screwed up, he'll think so, too." He'd bet that regret was already eating at Bedford like a cancer. Guys that arrogant thought they could have it all—beautiful wife, slutty mistress and whatever else money could buy. If he hadn't come to his senses yet, he soon would. When he did, would he try to get Leslie to take him back?

And would she fall for it?

Brent wanted to believe she was too sensible for that, even though it was none of his business. Had nothing to do with him at all. He'd keep her here as long as he could, but once she was ready to go back home and face the world, they'd go back to being casual acquaintances. She'd ignore him if she ran into him at the deli, or avoid him altogether.

Coping with that would be easier if she didn't get back together with Gerald. Since he couldn't tell her that, he decided it was time to change the subject.

"I still have to deliver that lumber to a job site and take the truck back to the warehouse."

"Are you taking Max with you?"

"I can if you want me to."

"No, leave him here. He's good company. I promise I won't feed him again. Is there anything else I'm not supposed to do?"

Brent scratched the dog behind the ears. "He's pretty tough. Aren't you, boy?"

Max panted in agreement.

Brent remembered what his mother had said earlier. *What about toiletries?* He'd rather not have to make another trip to the drugstore but if Leslie needed something, he'd get it for her. "Do you need me to pick up anything for you?"

"I'll be fine."

He suspected she was going easy on him, and he had no argument with that. "You can put your things in the spare room," he said. "Make yourself at home."

"Thanks. I really appreciate everything you've done."

Be interesting to see if she still felt that away after she saw what was in the bag. "I guess I should pick up something for dinner, too. Do you like pizza? Or Chinese?"

"Chinese would be great. Do you get it from Wong's Kitchen?"

"Isn't it the only Chinese restaurant in town?"

"I guess it is. I don't eat a lot of takeout but I do like their curried noodles."

"One of my favorites, too. What else would you like?"

"I'll leave that up to you. Surprise me."

Mr. Wong's menu had all the usual standards. No surprises there. Leslie would definitely be surprised that Brent wasn't over his high school crush, though. Hell, even he was caught off guard because until today, he'd been pretty sure he was.

You might be able to fool yourself, but you can't fool me. His mother was right. He wasn't fooling anybody. Least of all himself. He wasn't over her, and he probably never would be.

As SOON AS Brent pulled out of the driveway, Leslie checked her voice mail again. Five more calls. This time only one person hadn't left a message. Nick had returned hers and said to let him know if she needed anything. Her mother had called again, this time with a harsher reprimand and a reminder that if she wasn't going through with the wedding, she would have to return all the gifts. Leslie punched the key to delete it.

Two more from Allison, whose worried tone had escalated to annoyed. "I know you're checking your messages, Leslie. Why won't you call me?" and "I'm sending John over to your place again. I can't believe you're making us worry like this."

She banged the receiver back into its cradle a little harder than she needed to. "Damn it, Allison. This is *not* about you."

But she knew everyone, with the exception of her brother, would make this their business. Thank God she didn't have to go home and deal with the phone calls and people dropping by to check up on her.

She picked up the bag of clothing Brent had brought for her and carried it into his spare room. As she emptied the contents onto the bed, Max jumped up and flopped down next to them. The teddy bear immediately caught her attention. Max's, too.

"Hey," she said, snatching it out of his reach. "You have your own bear. Brent gave this one to me." She picked it up and for a few seconds, tears blurred her vision. Early that morning a courier had delivered Gerald's wedding gift. The diamond necklace and matching earrings were stunning, but they hadn't triggered any kind of emotional response. Maybe because she'd been expecting them. Not those exact pieces, but she'd known he would give her something extravagant.

The teddy bear was unexpected, and kind of sweet. Most men sent flowers when they were trying to make a woman feel better but it was becoming apparent that Brent wasn't like most men, at least not the ones she knew. She set the bear against the pillow and wiped her eyes on the sleeve of his T-shirt.

"I'll call him Max." The dog looked up at her. "That seems like a good name for my teddy bear, don't you think?" When her life was back to normal and she was back in her own home, she would still have Max the teddy bear as a reminder of being rescued by Brent and being here.

She turned her attention to the clothes. He'd really been concerned they might not be good enough for her. He also thought Gerald wasn't good enough for her, and she liked that. So, no matter what Brent had given her, she would not hurt his feelings by being anything but appreciative.

The jeans looked to be her size, so she wriggled out of Brent's sweat pants and pulled them on. They were pretty much a perfect fit, just snug enough to be flattering, and soft and faded enough to be comfortable. She hadn't been sure what he'd bring for her, but she hadn't expected anything quite this wearable. She decided to leave on his T-shirt, though, and save the other things for the next few days.

Could she stay that long? She was certainly in no hurry to face her family and friends, and in even less of a hurry to tell them about Gerald and Candice.

She picked up the pink toothbrush and opened the package. There was no place to store it in the bedroom so she took it into the bathroom.

While she'd been in the bath, she hadn't paid much attention to her surroundings. Brent had done a great job of renovating the bathroom while keeping some of the old fixtures and maintaining the heritage feel of the small home. The vanity was an old washstand with a sink installed in it. She loved antiques, and converting it had been a clever idea. A shelf above the sink held a plastic holder with one toothbrush. A blue one. She stuck her new pink one in next to it.

Gerald had kept a toothbrush at her town house but the en suite bathroom had a long, marble-topped vanity with two sinks, so his things were separate from hers. Here, the two toothbrushes stood with their handles crossed and their bristles facing each other. Like they belonged together. She quickly pulled hers out and set it on the shelf. Somehow the two toothbrushes together seemed way too personal.

She was about to leave the bathroom when she spotted her jewelry beside the sink. She scooped up the pieces, but one of the earrings slipped out of her palm.

She grabbed for it and missed. "Damn it!" she said as it slithered down the drain.

She peered into the opening and saw it was partly blocked

by two cross pieces. If she had any kind of luck the earring would have caught on one of them, but this was not her lucky day. The earring was gone.

She opened the doors of the vanity and pushed aside a stack of toilet paper so she could see the pipes. She had no idea what she was looking for, but she supposed the earring would be caught in the lowest part of the curved pipe. When Brent came home, she'd ask about calling a plumber.

She could always forget about the earring. It wasn't as if she would ever wear it again.

Would Gerald expect her to return the jewelry? Knowing him, he probably would. Well, he could think again. She could take them back to the store and get something more practical. Something she'd actually wear, something that wouldn't remind her that she'd almost ruined her life. Except anything she bought with that money would be a reminder that she nearly had. Better to do the right thing and return the jewelry.

And that meant asking Brent to help her get the earring out of the drain.

"What the hell," she said to her reflection in the mirror. "What's one more favor?"

She put the necklace and the other earring in the top drawer of the little dresser in the bedroom. While she was standing there, the phone rang. She ran into the kitchen to check the caller ID. C. Girling, again. "Oh, buzz off," she said to the phone. "If he wanted to talk to you, he would have called you back an hour ago."

She went back to the bedroom to finish putting her things away.

After she folded the shirts and set them inside a drawer, she held the nightgown up to herself. It was made of thin, pale-blue cotton, a little on the short side but otherwise fairly practical. Very much the sort of thing that was meant for sleeping in. It couldn't have been more different from the seductive pink silk number she'd intended to wear tonight. She quickly folded the nightgown, set it next to the shirts and closed the drawer.

The only other thing in the bag was a pair of sandals. She slipped off Brent's socks and tried them on. Not a brand name she recognized, but they were leather and very comfortable. They were new and only a half size too big. Perfect, really, considering that her only other options were either the socks or the wedding shoes she'd left by the front door.

She could use another set of underwear but as welcome as they would have been, she was grateful she didn't have to accept panties from a man she barely knew. If she washed the things she was wearing and hung them up before she went to bed, they would be dry by morning.

Max appeared to have fallen asleep, but he suddenly sat up as though listening for something and then leaped off the bed and raced out of the room. A minute later she heard Brent's key in the front door.

He was in the kitchen when she caught up with him, removing take-out containers from a large paper bag. The scents had her mouth watering. "That smells so good."

"I picked up a few groceries, too, so we'll have something for breakfast."

She hadn't thought that far ahead. Gerald was the only man she'd ever had breakfast with and the thought of waking up in the morning and having breakfast with Brent made her feel strangely self-conscious.

"Pull up a stool," he said. "I'll grab some plates."

"And then after we've eaten, I think we'll have to call a plumber."

He set the last container on the counter and looked at her. "Oka-a-ay. Why?"

"I left my earrings on the vanity in the bathroom and one

of them kind of went down the drain." *Like my marriage,* she thought, swallowing the laughter rising in the back of her throat.

"Those were beautiful earrings," he said.

"You mean it's gone?"

"Oh, it's still down there." He looked way too amused by this.

"So if we call a plumber, he'll be able to get it out for me?"

"Not necessary."

That sounded encouraging. "You know how to get things out of drains?"

"Piece of cake. Did you run any water after you dropped it?"

"No."

"Good. I'll grab a couple of tools and be right back."

All sorts of tempting aromas rose from the take-out containers lined up on the counter. She felt a little light-headed, she was so hungry. "We could leave it till after we eat."

"How much did those earrings cost?"

She shrugged. "A lot?"

"We'll get it now." He went out the back door and disappeared into a small shed. A few minutes later he was back with a red plastic bucket and a handful of tools.

She followed him to the bathroom. "Is there something I can do to help?"

He gave her two tools. "Sure. You can hand these to me when I need them."

She took the tools and stood back while he opened the vanity and emptied it. Then he set the bucket under the sink.

"Pass me that small wrench."

She knelt on the floor and gave him the smaller of the two tools she was holding, which turned out to be the right one because he used it to unscrew something from the underside of the pipe. Some gray-colored sludge drained into the bucket.

Max squeezed into the tiny bathroom, nearly knocking her over. She grabbed Brent's shoulder to steady herself.

He glanced back at her and the oversized dog. "I should have put him outside."

"I can do that," Leslie offered. But before she had a chance to move, Max jumped into the bathtub.

"He's fine in there," Brent said. "At least he's out of the way." He swirled the crud that had drained into the bucket. "It must still be caught in the trap," he said. He got down on the floor on his back, wedged his shoulders between the open doors of the vanity and angled his head under the sink.

She had no idea what kind of trap he was talking about.

With one hand he groped for a tool and grabbed her knee instead. "Sorry. I need the other wrench."

She handed him the only other tool she had. "That doesn't look like a wrench."

"Basin wrench." It clanged against the pipe and his biceps flexed as he wedged it into position. He heaved on it a couple of times and his T-shirt strained against his chest, then finally rode up, exposing hard, tanned abs. Very hard. Very nice. She tried to look away, but her eyes seemed to have a different idea.

Max leaned out of the tub and nudged her shoulder. *Good dog,* she thought. *I needed a distraction.*

Brent loosened some rings on the pipes and the curvy piece came away. He shoved himself out of the vanity, sat up and squinted as he looked into one end of the pipe. Then he tipped it her way so she could have a look. "There it is."

As he scrambled to his feet, she jumped up and took a step backward. Max got to his feet, too, but he stayed in the bathtub. Brent set the bucket in the tub under the faucet and turned on a trickle of water, letting it run into the pipe.

The dog stuck his nose under the stream.

"Come on, Max. Out of the way."

The dog stepped back but kept an eye on the water running from the tap.

Leslie watched as the grungy water flowed slowly out the

end of the pipe. When the earring appeared, Brent caught it in his fingers and held it up for her to see, then he rinsed it under the tap and handed it to her. "Good thing we found it. It'd be a shame to lose all those diamonds."

The sudden sharpness in his voice surprised her. "They were a gift from Gerald," she said, holding it in her palm, still a little reluctant to touch it after seeing where it had been. "I'm going to give them back."

"Then it's a good thing you didn't lose it."

That was true. "Nothing is going right today. I'm usually not this much trouble."

His eyes seemed to soften. "Leslie, you're no trouble. Besides, it doesn't hurt to clean out the trap once in a while."

"Is it called that because it traps things that fall down the drain?"

"Afraid not. Every time you turn on the tap, most of the water runs through the system but some of it always stays behind in this bend. That water closes off the pipe so gas from the sewer doesn't come up into the house."

"That is *really* disgusting."

He laughed. "Not as disgusting as a house full of sewer gas."

That was true. "I don't think I've ever had a conversation like this."

"And I've never had to fish diamonds out of a drainpipe. I guess that makes us even."

"Actually, I owe you for this. For everything."

"Next time I need something, I'll know who to ask."

For the first time that day he sounded like the guy she'd known in high school, always quick with a comeback and a double meaning. It had bugged her in those days, but right now she didn't mind playing along. "You can ask, but that doesn't mean you'll get what you want."

"I'm well aware of that, but sometimes persistence pays off."

His gaze held hers like a magnet. She couldn't have looked

away if she'd tried, and the walls of the tiny bathroom seemed to close in on them. She might have been tempted to continue the game if he hadn't just let on that her being here had something to do with his persistence. She had assumed his driving by the church had been a coincidence, but what if it wasn't? If that was the case, it definitely wouldn't be right to lead him on, and she always did the right thing.

Brent lightly touched her shoulder and urged her toward the door, then bent to pick up the tools. "Dinner's getting cold," he said softly. "I'll put the plumbing back together while you serve it. Plates are in the cupboard next to the fridge."

It was as if he'd sensed her confusion and was giving her an easy way out. She took it.

Chapter Four

Leslie set out two plates, the take-out boxes and the chopsticks. She was putting away the groceries when Brent came into the kitchen. He set the bucket and tools on the porch and closed the French doors. When he turned around and looked at her, the kitchen suddenly felt as small as the bathroom.

"Um, I guess we're ready to eat," she said.

"Would you like a glass of wine with dinner?" he asked. "I bought white. I hope that's okay."

"Thanks. I'd love some. Do you mind if I use your phone to check my messages?"

"You can use the phone anytime you like." He opened and closed one drawer, then another, and finally produced a corkscrew. "I knew I had one of these somewhere. You expecting an important call?"

"Not really. I just wondered if people are still looking for me."

"I think it's safe to say they are. Do you plan to return the calls?"

She shook her head.

"Then why don't you leave the messages till you're ready to deal with them?"

Good question. "In case you're wondering, I'm not checking to see if Gerald called."

"You think he would?" Brent uncorked the bottle and took a wineglass out of a cupboard.

She shrugged. "Someone called earlier, twice, and hung up."

He glanced up at her.

"I checked my messages while you were out. I'm sure it wasn't him, though."

"Right." He gestured toward the phone. "Be my guest."

"Thanks." But as soon as she heard the eight new messages and deleted them, she wished she hadn't checked. For one thing, she knew Brent could probably hear them, too. Four were from Allison, who said she'd sent her husband to Leslie's place three times to see if she was there. She might never go home if it meant having to deal with people calling incessantly and showing up at her door.

As she deleted the last message, she watched Brent pour wine into the glass. After she hung up, he handed it to her.

"Aren't you having any?" she asked.

"Not a big fan." He grabbed a bottle of beer from the fridge, twisted off the cap and touched the rim to her wineglass. He opened a drawer and took out a fork and then, almost as an afterthought, grabbed a beer glass from the same cupboard the wineglass had been in.

"Speaking of messages, you had another call while you were out," she said, catching herself before telling him it was the same person who'd called earlier.

He glanced at the phone and back at her. "Probably nothing important. I'll listen to the messages later." If he had already checked to see who called, he wasn't letting on. "Let's eat."

Leslie hadn't eaten all day and she was famished. After they'd both filled their plates, she picked up a piece of chicken and popped it into her mouth. "This is delicious."

Brent nodded in agreement as he chewed the forkful of chow mein he had just shoveled into his mouth.

"You don't use chopsticks?" she asked.

"Never did get the hang of them," he said as he loaded his fork again. "Besides, it takes too long to eat with those things."

She peeled the paper wrapper off the second set of chopsticks. "Would you like me to show you?"

He looked uncertain.

She handed them to him. "Just give it a try."

"You're really going to make me use these things?"

"It's up to you." She picked up her chopsticks, pretending not to notice that he watched her position them between her fingers and then tried to copy her. She twirled some of the curried noodles onto the end of hers and casually raised them to her mouth. "Delicious."

His silent struggle with the implements made her smile. "They're not wrenches," she said.

He was not amused.

"If you hold them lightly, they'll work much better for you." She set hers on the edge of her plate. "Let me show you." She placed his chopsticks into his hand and curled his fingers into position. "You only need to move one of them. Let the other one rest in your hand like this." His skin was tanned and warm and a little rough in places.

She looked up and was startled by the dark intensity in his eyes. She quickly let go and took up her chopsticks again.

"Don't try to eat anything yet. Just move them…like this."

He shifted his gaze to the implements in his hand and made a few awkward movements with them. "My food is getting cold."

She laughed. "You never know when a skill like this will come in handy."

"Like when there's a global fork shortage?"

"Very funny. You might be invited to dinner sometime and chopsticks will be the only things provided."

He stared at her. "In Collingwood Station? Who would invite people to dinner and only give them chopsticks?"

She smiled at him. "I would, if I was serving Japanese or Thai food."

"You would do that to people?"

"It's good food."

"I'm talking about the chopsticks."

"It's more authentic, and you get to eat slowly and savor every mouthful."

"I'll take your word for it." He moved the chopsticks a few more times. "Am I ready to graduate to actually eating with these things, or do I need more practice?"

"I'd say you still need a lot of practice," she said, surprising herself by the flirtatious tone in her voice. "But the more you eat, the better you'll get at it."

"Now there's something I don't hear often enough."

She laughed and handed his fork to him. "If you're really starving, why don't you use this?"

"You think I'm a quitter?"

"No. I think you're one of the most persistent people I've ever met."

He narrowed his eyes at her, picked up a piece of chicken and dropped it. On the second try he got it almost to his lips before the chopsticks twisted out of control. "Damn," he said as the meat fell back onto his plate.

She laughed. "You almost had it."

He gave her a bland look. "I'm also starving, and there's no almost about it." But he gave it one more try and that time he held on long enough to get the chicken into his mouth.

"See how easy that was?"

He raised one eyebrow at her while he made a production of chewing and swallowing, as though it might be the last thing he ever ate.

"If you're in a hurry, you can always use your fork."

"No hurry at all. Would you like more wine?"

Why not? "I'd love some."

He refilled her glass and got another beer for himself.

An hour later, Leslie glanced at the clock and couldn't believe the time had slipped by so quickly. She felt relaxed, and she was actually having fun. Or maybe that was the wine? Whatever was responsible for her current mood, it came as surprise. As did Brent's newfound proficiency with the chopsticks.

"The next time I serve Thai food at a dinner party, I'll invite you." That *definitely* had to be the wine talking.

"Who else do you usually invite?" he asked.

Interesting question. Gerald and his friends were definitely off any future guest list, as was Candice. "Maybe I'll invite Nick and his friend Maggie. Did you know she was his date for the wedding?"

Brent nodded.

"I think she's good for him. My brother deserves to have a wonderful person in his life." Leslie finished her wine. Was that the second glass? The third?

"Everybody does."

"What about you?" she asked.

"What about me?"

"Do you have someone wonderful in your life?" She immediately regretted the question. Definitely too much wine. "I'm sorry. Your personal life is none of my business."

"No problem. And no, there's no one wonderful right now. But I'd like to hear more about this dinner party. So far there's you, me, Nick and Maggie. That sounds more like a double date."

She felt her face heat up. "Or friends having dinner together. Or you could bring a date."

He lounged back in his chair, a smile slowly spreading across his face. "I just told you I'm not seeing anyone."

Which meant he *wasn't* seeing Cathy Girling. "You said there was no one wonderful."

"I wouldn't see anyone who wasn't."

"What about Cappuccino Girl? Was she someone special?"

Oh my God, Leslie thought, wishing she could grab the words and stuff them back inside her mouth. *How could you ask him something like that?* She glanced at the half-empty wine bottle and tried to cover her flaming-hot cheeks with her hands. "I'm sorry. I think I've had too much to drink."

"Who is Cappuccino Girl?" He sounded confused.

And why wouldn't he be. "She's nobody."

Brent's eyebrows went up a notch.

"Okay, she's someone I saw you with at the deli when I first moved back to town. She was…drinking cappuccino."

"Right." His mouth curved into a slow, lazy smile. "I remember that day. I don't think you stopped to say hello, did you?"

No, she had grabbed her bag and run. "You looked…busy."

"Did I?" His amusement was really starting to bug her. "To answer your question, she was no one special. And I'm not still seeing her. In case you were wondering."

Leslie looked down at her empty plate and fidgeted with her chopsticks. "I wasn't," she said. The only thing she was wondering was how an innocent invitation to a dinner party could have landed her in such dangerous territory.

"You know, Nick's never mentioned that he was a regular at your dinner parties."

"It's too bad that he and I went our separate ways after I went away to college. I wish I'd never let that happen."

Brent was watching her like a detective.

"We seem to have reconnected in the past few weeks, with the wedding plans and everything, so I think a dinner party is in order."

"And you promise there'll be chopsticks?" He took hers out of her hand and even in her wine-induced daze, she sensed that his hands lingered a little longer than necessary.

And then, although she was sure neither of them had

moved, his mouth seemed closer than it had a moment ago. Was he going to kiss her? Or…had she almost kissed him?

This was crazy.

"More wine?" he asked.

She put a hand over her glass. "No! Thanks, but no."

"You should go sit in the living room," he said quietly. "I'll tidy up in here and join you in a few minutes."

She nodded mutely. Normally she would offer to help, but she needed a few minutes to herself.

AFTER Leslie left the kitchen, Brent put the leftovers in the refrigerator. He should be feeling guilty for pouring that last glass of wine for her, but then she might never have said anything about the woman at the deli. For the life of him he couldn't remember who was with him, but he remembered Leslie. He hadn't seen her in a few years, and she had looked more beautiful and sure of herself than ever. She'd always been fiercely independent, and he'd always loved that about her. While the other girls had flirted and dressed to get the attention of every guy in school, Leslie had been her own person.

Trying to recall the identity of Cappuccino Girl had him smiling again. If he didn't know better, he'd think Leslie had been jealous.

He scraped the plates and dumped them into the sink, but he hesitated before letting go of the chopsticks. He set Leslie's on the counter and his next to them. Keeping them seemed ridiculously sentimental but tossing them wasn't an option. Not yet. Something had happened a few minutes ago—electrifying moments filled with promise and uncertainty—and he liked the prospect of more chopsticks in their future.

When he went in the living room, Leslie was curled up at one end of the sofa, legs tucked beneath her and her head resting against the back, eyes closed. Max sprawled beside her, his head on her lap.

Lucky dog.

She was stroking the top of his head with one hand, so she wasn't asleep.

It was getting hard to remember that she didn't belong here, and she wasn't staying. He sat at the other end of the sofa. "Leslie?"

She opened her eyes and gave him a sleepy look. "I hope it's okay for Max to be up here. I didn't have the heart to make him get down."

"He does whatever he wants when I'm not here so I've given up trying to make him stay off the furniture."

She smiled and her eyelids slid shut again.

"You're exhausted," he said. "You should get some sleep. The bed in the spare room is already made up."

She opened her eyes and yawned. "Thanks. I didn't get much sleep last night and it's been a long day."

Even from his perspective, calling this a long day was an understatement. She seemed to be handling everything remarkably well, even for her. Maybe too well? But then, theatrics had never been her style.

He watched her ease Max's head off her leg and stand up.

"Do you need anything?" he asked.

She shook her head. "I'll just brush my teeth and go to bed." At the archway that led to the hall, she stopped and turned around. "Thanks for everything you've done for me. I really appreciate it." She covered another yawn with her hand before she disappeared into the bedroom and closed the door.

Brent went back into the kitchen and opened the French doors for Max. "Out you go." While he waited, he picked up the phone and punched in the code to retrieve his messages.

There were two, both from his friends Cathy and Dave.

"Hey, Brent. Have you heard the news? Leslie Durrance left Gerald Bedford standing at the altar this morning. Haven't heard what happened but I take it she's back on the market. Give us a call when you get a chance."

Brent rolled his eyes at the ceiling.

He heard Leslie come out of the bedroom and go into the bathroom. Leslie Durrance was in his bathroom, brushing her teeth with a toothbrush he'd bought for her. He didn't know about her being back on the market, but Gerald Bedford was history, and Leslie suddenly didn't seem to mind Brent's company. Still, he did not need any interference.

He listened to the second message.

"Hey, it's Cathy again. Dave and I were wondering if you'd like to come over for a barbecue tonight. Thought we'd give Nick and his new girlfriend a call, too. See if we can get the lowdown on Leslie. Let us know if you're free."

Luckily she hadn't called while he was here. Leslie would have thought it strange if he didn't answer, but Cathy's voice could fill a room, even through the telephone, and Leslie would not react well to the idea of "being back on the market."

He picked up her chopsticks in one hand and his in the other, and tapped them together. Who knew? Maybe the old Brent had a shot with the new Leslie.

Yeah, right. The earring he'd fished out of the plumbing had to have cost a small fortune, and yet she hadn't seemed concerned about losing it. If he had told her it was gone for good, he didn't think she would have cared.

He had a comfortable life but even if he cleaned out his savings account and maxed out his credit cards, he couldn't afford to buy things like that for her. Never mind the engagement ring she'd been wearing. Which she no longer had on, he'd noticed. It must be in the bedroom with her other things. At least she was in no danger of losing that.

The water stopped running in the bathroom. Several minutes later, he heard the bathroom door open and the bedroom door close.

He went over to the French doors and whistled for Max, who bounded inside and immediately went in search of Leslie. Brent locked the door and followed.

Max sat outside her bedroom, nose pressed against the narrow space between the door and the floor. "Are you keeping an eye on her?" Brent asked quietly from the doorway to his own bedroom.

Max looked back at him and then flopped onto the floor against the door as though trying to tell him that no one, not even him, was getting to Leslie.

"Like I'd even try," he whispered. He glanced at his watch. Not yet ten o'clock. He didn't want to turn on the television in case it kept her awake. Maybe he'd read for a while, but first he needed a shower. He should have done that after he'd unloaded the lumber, but he'd been distracted by taking apart the plumbing and learning how to use chopsticks.

He went into the bathroom, closed the door and stripped off his clothes. The room held a faint scent of woman, and he reacted to it immediately. Damn it.

He drew the curtain around the tub and turned on the water. A few minutes alone in the shower was no substitute for a night in bed with the one woman he'd always wanted and had never been able to have, but it wasn't like that was going to happen, anyway. Not this night, and certainly not with that woman. On the bright side, the woman of his dreams *was* in his spare bedroom and that was something he'd never thought possible. Maybe if he played his cards right…

Leslie wasn't like most other women, though. Hell, she wasn't like *any* other woman, and he didn't just want to sleep with her. He wanted it all. Making love to her now would only make getting over her a hundred times harder than it had been ten years ago.

Speaking of hard…he stepped into the tub and stood under

the warm spray for a few seconds. Think about something else, he told himself. Anything but Leslie.

He reached for the soap and ran the bar across his chest. Something sharp grazed his skin, then clanged to the bottom of the tub. He caught a flash of light as the object skittered toward the drain. He jabbed one foot over the opening, a split second after the damn thing disappeared. He hadn't actually seen it but he knew exactly what it was. Leslie's engagement ring.

"You have got to be freaking kidding me," he said. He cranked off the taps and stared down the drain.

Damn it. This could not be happening.

Maybe it hadn't been the ring. Surely to God she wouldn't leave something that valuable in the soap dish.

Yes, she would.

His irritation dampened the enthusiasm he'd been feeling a minute ago. He stepped out of the tub, wrapped a towel around his waist and flung the door open.

Max, in his newly self-appointed role as guard dog, raised his head.

Brent was relieved to see a band of light still shining from under the door. "Leslie?" He hoped it didn't sound as though he was shouting.

The rustle of sheets was followed by a faint, "Yes?"

"Where's your engagement ring?" he asked, knowing his voice transmitted his annoyance.

He heard her footsteps cross the floor, then the door opened a crack. "I left it…" She paused, as though trying to remember where she'd put it. "Oh, it's in the soap dish in the bathtub."

"No, it isn't."

The door opened wider. The nightgown he'd brought for her was a little shorter and a lot more transparent than it needed to be. Her long, slender legs might have been distracting if her nipples weren't nudging at the fabric.

Here we go again, he thought. He hoped she wouldn't

notice the movement under his towel. But her eyes widened and her color heightened, indicating she had.

He thought about how much it would cost to replace the ring if the thing had already made its way to the sewer. Ah yes, that did the trick.

"What happened to it?" she asked. Then her eyes lit up with amusement. "No! You didn't!"

"Yes, I did. How is that funny?"

"It isn't."

But obviously she thought it was. "Come on, Leslie—"

"It's kind of symbolic," she said, still smiling.

He couldn't stop himself from rolling his eyes. Symbolic or not, thousands of dollars' worth of diamonds down the drain—his drain, dropped down there by him—was no laughing matter.

She sobered slightly. "You didn't have any trouble finding my earring."

"It helped that the trap was right there under the sink."

"Where's the trap for the bathtub?"

"In the crawl space under the house."

"Oh."

He could see that she had no idea what that meant. "You'd better get dressed. I'm going to need help."

"Can't it wait till tomorrow?"

"Not if I'm going to get any sleep tonight."

LESLIE STRIPPED off the nightgown and dragged Brent's shirt over her head. A crawl space didn't sound like the kind of place she wanted to wear her new jeans, and her just-washed underwear was hanging in the closet, so she had no choice but to pull on Brent's sweat pants over bare skin.

Her head was starting to hurt and all she wanted to do was sleep. Between the exhaustion and too much wine, she could hardly think straight. Brent's wet body, scantily clad in a towel, had her feeling even more muddled. She slipped her feet into the sandals he'd given her and opened the bedroom door.

Brent was waiting. He hadn't dried off before getting dressed and his T-shirt clung damply to his chest. He seemed to be completely unaware of the effect his body had on her, otherwise she might think he'd done it on purpose.

Now that they were dressed, she felt a little more composed. She had been unprepared for his naked torso, still shimmering wet from the shower. Not that there was any way to prepare for something like that. Physical labor did amazing things for a man's body and the more she saw, the more she liked.

"Ready?" he asked.

She nodded. The sooner this was over, the sooner she could crawl back into bed and get some sleep. And clear the images of Brent in a towel out of her mind, she thought as she followed him through the kitchen and out the French doors onto the porch. He grabbed the bucket and the tools he'd left there earlier and pulled two ball caps off a hook and a flashlight from the shelf above. Then he flipped a light switch, dimly illuminating a small semicircle of the backyard. "Watch your step."

She had stopped watching her step the moment she'd climbed into his truck that morning. It seemed a little late to start now.

He shone the flashlight at the back of the house at ground level. She had no idea what he was looking for until he reached down and unlatched a small panel. It was actually a door, maybe three feet high, and it swung open on creaky hinges. He crouched near the opening and shone the light under the house.

She knelt beside him and looked inside. "You have to go in there?" she asked.

"*We* have to. I'll need you to hold the flashlight for me."

The thought of crawling into that dark space made her skin itch. "You don't think there are spiders in there, do you?"

He hesitated, as if trying to figure out what his answer should be. "No," he said. "Probably not."

"Liar." The place was probably teeming with all kinds of creepy crawlies.

He placed the cap he was carrying on her head, backwards.

"What's that for?"

"To keep the cobwebs out of your hair."

"You just said there wouldn't be spiders."

"You won't see them if there are. Too dark."

"That's no consolation."

"I didn't imagine it would be."

"But you're still making me go in."

"It'll be just as dark and spooky under there in the morning as it is now. And I don't think I should have to do this alone. You're the one who left the ring lying around."

All valid points. "So if I say you shouldn't worry about the ring—"

"Don't even think about it."

"I'm too busy thinking about spiders."

"Try not to."

Oh, sure. Like that was going to happen.

He handed the flashlight to her and got down on his hands and knees. "Ready?"

No, but she nodded anyway.

He crawled through the opening, pushing the bucketful of tools ahead of himself. After his butt disappeared into the darkness, she held her breath and followed.

Chapter Five

Now she knew why it was called a crawl space. The air had an earthy smell but in spite of all the rain that morning, this place was bone-dry. And even with the narrow cone of light coming from the flashlight, it was too dark to see the spiders, though she knew they were there.

Please don't let one of those things walk on me.

"Can you shine that over here?" Brent asked.

She angled the light in his direction. He hadn't gone very far, and he was looking up at some plumbing.

"I need you to hold it close to the pipe so I can see what I'm doing."

That she could do. But as she moved closer, the invisible strands of a spiderweb stuck to her face. She dropped the flashlight with a thud and tried to wipe the revoltingly sticky strands off her skin.

Brent picked up the flashlight.

"Sorry," she said. "I have a serious spider phobia."

"Didn't they make a movie about that?"

She shuddered. "If they did, I didn't see it."

He laughed softly and brushed her cheek with his thumb. "There. It's gone. Ready to get to work?"

His touch took her by surprise, partly because that wasn't where the spiderweb had stuck to her. She'd had no trouble fending him off in high school, and it might be easier now if she hadn't had too much to drink. Back then she'd thought he was good-looking—she hadn't been *that* different from the other girls—but until today she'd never actually felt attracted to him.

"What do you want me to do?" she asked.

"Hold the light?" He handed it back to her.

Of course. She directed the beam at the pipes but it illuminated his face, too. He was smiling, as if he'd suddenly come to the same realization she had.

Leslie Durrance has the hots for Brent Borden.

No, she doesn't.

For heaven's sake, what's wrong with you? she asked herself.

Brent took a closer look at the plumbing and sighed.

"Something wrong?"

He shook his head. "Doesn't look good. These old cast-iron pipes are pretty badly corroded."

"So we're done?"

"I'm persistent, remember?"

She swatted at something crawling on the back of her hand. "How long is this going to take?"

"If all goes well? Five or ten minutes."

She didn't ask how long it would take if things didn't go well. She didn't want to know.

Brent fitted a wrench to one of the pipes and heaved on it. Nothing happened, although the sound of metal on metal got Max's attention. He ran through the house, barking, and the sound of his paws on bathroom floor could be heard directly overhead.

"Great," Brent said. "I should have realized this would make him nuts. The neighbors will wonder what's going on." He braced one shoulder against the outside wall and had another go at the pipe. Judging by his groaning, this was not going to be easy.

"Feel free to swear at it if you want," she said.

"If I thought it would help, I would." He squirted some oily-smelling stuff around the places where the pipes were connected.

"What's that?" she asked.

"Lubricant. I'll give it a minute or two and see if it does the trick."

She watched him examine the pipes. He was a lot like her brother, which was probably why they'd stayed such good friends for so many years.

He glanced at her and smiled.

She smiled back, then quickly lowered the flashlight, hoping he wouldn't notice.

He wrapped his hand gently around her wrist and redirected the light. She knew it was so he could see her, but the light also defined the angles of his face—the well-proportioned nose and a firm jaw that had gone a little too long without being shaved. She wondered how it felt.

"Are you and Nick still working on Maggie's house?" she blurted out, thinking that inane conversation might help keep her mind, and her hands, off him.

"We finished yesterday. He was in a hurry to get things wrapped up so he could, ah, take her to your wedding."

"I hope things work out for them. This morning she certainly helped me figure out what to do."

"How?"

"I might have gone through with the wedding if I hadn't run into her. She told me to listen to my heart."

Brent didn't say anything.

"Actually, I'll never forget what she said. 'Your head will always look for reasons to explain away the doubt, but it can never change what you know in your heart.' And she was right. Running away from the church was only possible because I didn't let myself think about the consequences."

"Good for her," Brent said, his voice barely audible.

Something tickled the back of Leslie's neck. She swiped at it and knocked the ball cap askew.

Brent reached out and straightened it. Then he pulled on a pair of worn work gloves and raised the wrench to the pipe again. "Okay, time to get serious."

The clatter set off Max's barking again.

"Crazy mutt," Brent muttered.

"He must be a good watch dog."

"Yeah, till the burglar gets inside and Max tries to get the guy to play with him."

Leslie laughed. "I can imagine that."

Brent grunted and heaved on the wrench again, and something moved. "That's more like it." It took him a few minutes to loosen the two metal rings that held the pipes together, but finally the curved part that he called the trap came away. He held it over the bucket and looked into one end of it. "Hand me the light," he said.

She did, and watched as he shone it into one end of the pipe. Max's barking had turned to whimpering.

"There it is." Brent turned the pipe upside down and banged it against the pail. Watery sludge dribbled out and the ring clanked into the bottom of the bucket. "Thank God." He pulled it out and wiped it on his shirt before he handed it to her.

The ring that had once given her so much pleasure now sat in the palm of her hand, and she felt absolutely nothing. The stupid thing must be jinxed, she decided, and she could not wait to give it back to Gerald. He could do whatever he wanted with it. Give it to Candice and let it work its black magic on her.

At least Brent could stop worrying about it.

She searched the sides of the sweat pants but there were no pockets.

"You should put it on," Brent said. "We don't want to lose it down here."

No way. She shook her head and handed it back to him. "I am never wearing that ring again. Put it in your pocket."

She could see he wasn't crazy about the idea, but he silently tucked it into the pocket of his jeans. He lifted the pipe back into position and then started to laugh. "Max, you goofy dog. What are you doing?"

"You can see him?"

"Yes. He's in the bathtub, looking down the drain and probably thinking we're the crazy ones."

Leslie laughed, too, and crawled closer. "Let me see."

Brent inched aside so she could move in and look up through the pipe. Sure enough, there was Max. She could only make out some of his fur and periodic glimpses of his dark, wet nose as it sniffed at the opening. "He's so funny. And he'd be right about us being the crazy ones."

She glanced at Brent and stopped laughing. He'd put a supporting arm around her shoulders while she leaned back to look up the drain. His face was only inches from hers, and she wanted to kiss him. Except there was no logical explanation for why she would do that, unless she blamed it on the wine.

Listen to your heart, a voice inside her head said.

No way.

"Leslie?"

"Mmm?"

"You need to stop looking at me like that."

"Why?"

"I think you know why."

She certainly did. Next thing she knew, her lips touched his.

Whose idea had that been? Hers? Was she using him to make herself feel better about being cheated on? No. Maybe.

If he knew, he didn't seem to mind because he took control and then there was no more thinking.

His mouth was gentle but demanding and she parted her lips, expecting to feel the touch of his tongue. Instead he drew her bottom lip between his teeth, sucked it softly and released it. A few repetitions of that had her thinking about naked bodies and orgasms.

When he stopped, he was holding her face in both of his hands, she was clinging to his shoulders and Max was panting through the drainpipe.

Brent groped for the flashlight and put it in her hands. "Let's put this thing back together. I have a feeling we're both going to need a shower when we get out of here." He muttered something about his being a cold one.

What was wrong with her? She had more sense and self-control than this. "Brent, I'm so sor—"

"Stop."

"This is all Max's fault."

"You're kidding, right? It was what it was. Can you leave it at that?"

"And what was it?"

"Forget about it, okay?"

Like that was going to happen. If she didn't figure out why she had done something so impulsive, she might do it again. "I'm not like all the other women who throw themselves at you—"

"Goddamn it, Leslie. Don't ruin it."

"Don't shout at me. And you shouldn't have made me come down here."

"Give me a break." He slammed the pipe into place and started tightening the rings that held it together. "I'd forgotten how stubborn you are. You always did have to have the last word."

"That is totally unfair."

"No, that is called hitting the nail on the head." He heaved on the wrench one last time and tossed it into the bucket.

"Under the circumstances, I don't think you have any right to be upset."

"*Under the circumstances?* Let's see, where should I start?"

"I didn't mean *these* exact circumstances, per se."

Even in the dim light it was impossible to miss the exasperation in his eye roll. "Let the record show, Ms. Durrance, that *you* kissed *me*."

"It's not like you've never kissed me."

"The first time I tried, you punched me."

"I was eleven."

Apparently that was no defense because he ignored it and continued. "The next time, you turned around and walked away."

"Maybe I should have hit you that time, too."

He stopped what he was doing and looked directly at her. "And what about this time, Leslie? What did you feel like doing?"

More than kissing, that was for sure. Thankfully they'd been in this dark, dingy crawl space, surrounded by tools and spiders and dismantled plumbing. If they'd been upstairs, with him in a towel and her in the skimpy nightgown, she didn't even want to consider what she might have done. Stopped after one kiss? Not likely.

"Yeah," he said, as though he'd been reading her mind. "That's what I thought."

He went back to work, and she gripped the flashlight, willing herself to stop shaking. Finally he grabbed the bucket and the rest of his tools. "That's it," he said. "Let's get out of here."

Max's boisterous greeting at the back door did nothing to break the iciness between them. Inside the kitchen, Brent looked at her, quickly glanced at his hands and then back at her face. "We both need a shower," he said. "You go ahead."

His hands were grimy with grease and sludge from the drain. She touched her cheek where he'd touched her.

"I should have kept my hands to myself," he said softly.

Me, too. "I—" She wanted to apologize again, this time for blaming him for the kiss, but she didn't want to start another argument.

"Oh, before I forget." He dug the ring out of his jeans. "Better put this in a safe place."

"Thanks." For the first time since Gerald had given it to her, the diamonds seemed ridiculously large, almost obscene, and there were way too many of them. They had represented everything the two of them had wanted the rest of the world to believe about them, but absolutely nothing about their feelings for each other. She curled her fingers around it so neither of them had to look at it. The ring was warm from being in his pocket, and the warmth seeped into her palm.

She backed away, pointing over her shoulder. "I'd better go, um, have a shower and go to bed. To sleep."

In the bedroom she opened the top drawer of the dresser, set the ring inside with the other jewelry, and quickly shut it again. As soon as she was back at home, her first priority would be to return these things to Gerald.

She slipped off the sandals and picked up her nightgown. On her way from the bedroom to the bathroom, she heard Brent in the kitchen talking to Max.

"Leslie says it's your fault she kissed me," he said. "Good dog."

He must have thought she was already in the bathroom. She slipped inside, careful to close the door without making a sound. She didn't want him to know she'd heard him, but she was glad she had. Did he still have feelings for her?

Blaming the kiss on Max had been beyond silly, and it certainly hadn't been Brent's fault. None of this would have happened if the ring had stayed in the soap dish, or if Gerald had never given it to her in the first place.

She looked at herself in the mirror and ran the tip of a finger over the black smudges on her face. Grow up, she told herself. She'd never forgotten the way he'd kissed her on prom night. A girl never forgot her first kiss, and she remembered that one as though it were yesterday. It had been a teenage kiss with just a hint of tongue. She knew her inexperience had to be obvious and walking away had been the only way she knew to save face.

Tonight's kiss had been the grown-up kind that melted a woman's bones. "Admit it," she said to her reflection. "You loved it." If it ever happened again, she wouldn't make a scene. Except there couldn't be a next time. It wouldn't be fair to Brent.

LESLIE WOKE to the smell of coffee and bacon. After a few seconds of disorientation, she remembered where she was. Brent was already up and making breakfast.

She groaned and pulled the pillow over her head. She had made a complete fool of herself last night, first kissing him and then trying to make it his fault, Max's fault, anybody's fault but hers. He probably thought she was as crazy as a loon.

She shoved the pillow aside and stared up at the ceiling. So why had she kissed him last night? It was a good question with no logical answer. All she knew for sure was that if she tried it again, she had better be prepared for the consequences.

How she was going to face him over breakfast was the more urgent question, and there was no way to avoid it. "You can't stay in here all day," she said to herself. "The sooner you deal with this, the better."

She pushed back the covers and stretched. The bacon smelled wonderful, and she hadn't eaten it in years. Probably not since she'd lived at home. Hannah, their housekeeper, had always had time to make Leslie a plate of bacon and eggs over easy.

These days Leslie was more concerned about calories and cholesterol. Apparently Brent wasn't. She inhaled the heavenly scent again and smiled at the little teddy bear sitting on the nightstand.

"One piece isn't going to kill me." Even she didn't equate

eating bacon with living dangerously, but a person didn't change overnight. "Baby steps," she told herself. "You'll get there."

She slipped out of bed, pulled the nightgown over her head and opened the closet. Before going to bed last night she'd washed her bra and panties in the bathroom and hung them in there to dry. Luckily, they were. She pulled on the jeans and the pink T-shirt Brent had brought for her. It was her favorite color and although it was probably a coincidence, she was glad he had chosen it for her. She slipped her feet into the sandals and opened the bedroom door.

Max bounded into the room and dropped his teddy bear at her feet.

"I don't want your silly old bear." But she made a playful grab for it, and as expected he snatched it away from her and sped out of the room. She laughed at his antics and headed for the bathroom.

A few minutes later she made her way to the kitchen where Brent stood at the stove, a tall glass of orange juice in one hand and a spatula in the other. He was flipping bacon in a large cast-iron pan. He was in jeans and bare feet. His red T-shirt was just snug enough to draw her attention to the strength in his upper body.

He glanced at her over his shoulder. "Good morning. I hope Max didn't wake you."

"The bacon did. It smells great."

"It's supposed to be a scorcher today. Humid, too, so I thought I'd get ahead of the heat. I hope you like bacon and eggs."

"I love them. It was my favorite breakfast when I was growing up."

"Good, because it's one of the only things I know how to make." He forked the last piece out of the pan and onto a plate, then took a carton of eggs out of the fridge.

"How do you like yours?" he asked.

"Over easy," she said without hesitation, fighting the temptation to sneak a piece of bacon. It looked nice and crisp, just the way she liked it.

"One egg or two?"

"Just one. Can I help?"

"Everything's under control. Coffee's ready, though. Help yourself."

Apparently they were going to ignore what had happened last night, and that was fine with her. She watched him pour bacon fat from the pan into an empty soup can and tried not to think about her arteries. She poured herself a cup of coffee and a glass of juice, set them on the raised counter and climbed onto a stool. She usually made herself a latte in the morning.

A sip of Brent's coffee had her sputtering.

"Too strong?" he asked.

Too strong was an understatement. "A little stronger than I'm used to," she said, adding another generous splash of milk.

He laughed. "That's what everyone says."

Was *everyone* a reference to the other women who woke up here and ate Brent's bacon and eggs for breakfast? She glanced at the phone and saw that the message light was no longer blinking, which meant he'd listened to the messages from Cathy, or whoever C. Girling might be. Which was none of her business, she reminded herself.

She wondered how many more messages had accumulated since she'd checked hers last night.

"You okay?" Brent asked. He cracked an egg and sent it sputtering into the pan.

"I'm fine. Why?"

"I thought you might be worried about last night—"

So they *were* going to talk about it. "I'm not. I'm more worried about the number of people who keep trying to call me. Allison said she'd sent John over three times. I'm not ready to deal with them yet."

"Then don't." He made it sound easy.

"I hate to think what people must be saying about me."

He cracked three more eggs into the frying pan and concentrated on those while he spoke. "People are always going to talk and you can't do anything to stop them, so why worry about it?"

"Because they probably think this is my fault."

He looked at her then, intently and with purpose. "But you know it isn't, and the people who care about you will know it isn't. No one else is worth worrying about."

She watched him slide her egg onto a plate along with half the bacon and a slice of warm, buttered toast, and set it in front of her. He put three eggs, the rest of the bacon and three slices of toast on his plate.

"I'll try to keep that in mind," she said, eyeing his plate. "Are you really going to eat all that?"

"Every bite," he said with a satisfied grin, setting the plate on the counter next to hers. "You know you've done the right thing and that's all that really matters."

"In my head, I know that."

"But you're supposed to listen to your heart, remember?"

His reference to Maggie's advice made her smile. And he was right, of course. She knew Nick and Allison would support her, but she didn't even want to consider her mother's reaction. Would Lydia Durrance understand why she'd bolted from the church instead of going through with the wedding? Leslie was in no hurry to learn the answer to that question.

"I appreciate everything you've done for me. Do you mind if I stay another day or so?"

"You can stay as long as you like." He reached for the coffeepot and refilled their cups, then sat on the stool next to her. "So you think this is too strong?" he asked after he took a mouthful. "Tomorrow I'll let you make it."

"It's a deal. I'll even make breakfast."

"I'm guessing it'll be something better than bacon and eggs."

"Nothing's better than bacon and eggs." And he'd made hers just the way she liked them. "But my French toast is excellent."

"Sounds like another trip to the grocery store."

"Do you mind?"

"Are you kidding? I'd do more than that for a home-cooked breakfast. But you don't have to cook, you know."

"Since you've given me a place to stay, it's the least I can do. Besides, I love to cook."

"You do?"

"Yes. Does that surprise you?"

"No. Well, sort of. I mean, you and Nick grew up with cooks and housekeepers doing all that stuff for you."

"We did, but I left home years ago."

"I know you did."

"But you think I still have people looking after me?"

He tore a piece of toast in half and used it to mop up the egg yolk on his plate. He didn't answer, but she could tell what he was thinking. That she was still the spoiled little rich girl.

"FYI, I can look after myself. If I had to, I could even learn how to take apart plumbing."

Brent tipped his head back and laughed. "I was out of line. I'll bet you do an amazing job of everything, and I totally had that coming."

No, he hadn't, not this time, but with him she had always been on the defensive. "You don't have to apologize," she said.

"At least it seemed to cheer you up."

But when she caught a glimmer of the look he'd given her last night just before she kissed him, she stopped smiling. She quickly picked up her glass and drank the rest of the orange juice. When she glanced at him again, the look was gone. Maybe she'd imagined it.

The phone rang, startling both of them and breaking

whatever spell had started to weave itself in the narrow space between them.

Brent grabbed the phone and glanced at the call display, then looked at Leslie as he answered. "Hey, Mom. What's up?"

Chapter Six

Not wanting to listen in on their conversation, Leslie slid off her stool and stepped through the open French doors onto the porch. The backyard was nicely secluded by a tall fence and several large trees. Max was romping across the lawn in a vain attempt to catch a butterfly. She'd been there less than twenty-four hours and already she'd fallen completely in love with Max and his crazy antics. And while Brent was on the phone with his mother, Max provided an entertaining distraction.

Brent's mother knew she was here. Was she calling to check up on them?

Because Colleen Borden doesn't like you. Leslie had never been able to figure out why, but since she was no longer on the redevelopment committee, it hadn't mattered. Until now.

She was debating whether or not to join Max in the yard when Brent appeared.

"There's a flooding problem in the basement of the shelter. My mother doesn't know what's wrong, but I'm guessing it could be from all the rain yesterday. I should run over and take a look."

"That's fine. I'll stay here and wash the breakfast dishes."

"Sure. Or…" He hesitated. "You're welcome to come with me, if you feel like an outing. Sunday mornings are quiet, and we're only going to the shelter."

His unspoken meaning was clear. She didn't need to worry about running into anyone she knew at the homeless shelter. He was right about that, and she was feeling restless. Besides, she liked spending time with him and when she did, she hardly thought about Gerald. Ha. When she was with Brent, she didn't think about Gerald at all.

"It would be nice to get out for a while," she said.

"Good. If it turns out to be a plumbing problem, you can start your apprenticeship." His face had that characteristic flash of mischief that she remembered from when they were teenagers.

"You just need someone to hold your flashlight."

"You're pretty good at it."

She knew he was baiting her, and it was working. "I'm good at lots of things."

"That is true," he agreed.

"Being a perfectionist has its advantages."

"Ye-e-es," he said. "But…"

"But what?"

"You could use a little more practice."

Very funny, Brent Borden. Two can play this game, you know. "Practice. *You* are saying *I* need practice?"

He gave an expansive shrug. "They say it makes perfect."

She tried to act indignant but all she could do was laugh. What she really wanted to do was hug him for breaking the ice, but under these circumstances, physical contact wasn't a smart idea. "If I ever decide I need to be a better kisser, I'll let you know."

"I thought we were talking plumbing." His surprise was so convincing that she almost fell for it. And then his smile let her in on the joke.

"You're hopeless," she said.

He leaned close enough to touch her, but he didn't. She couldn't have torn her gaze from his if she'd tried. Not that she tried.

"I've been told I'm pretty good," he said. "Anytime you feel like more practice, give me a call."

That was classic Brent Borden, exactly the way she remembered him. "How long did you plan to ignore the flooding problem at the shelter?"

"Right. We should go," he said. "I'll put Max in the house and get my keys."

While he distracted Max and coaxed him inside with a doggie treat, Leslie went into the bathroom and looked at herself in the mirror. She combed her hair and smoothed her T-shirt. Without makeup, there wasn't much else she could do.

Would Colleen Borden like her better in hand-me-downs? Brent didn't seem to mind.

BRENT PARKED his pickup truck on the street in front of a rundown building. As they got out, he hoisted a toolbox out of the back and joined Leslie. She walked close to him as they approached the entrance and did her best to avoid the glassy-eyed stares of the men lounging on the sidewalk. She couldn't imagine what they had in their misshapen bundles and over-stuffed shopping carts, but those things were probably all they had in the world.

To her dismay, Brent stopped to talk to several of them. He even knew their names. She stood next to him, feeling awkward and out of place, and hating herself for it. After they'd discussed the weather and his reason for being there, he finally turned to her. "Come on," he said. "Let's go in and see what needs to be fixed."

He pushed a buzzer and waited.

A moment later a crackly male voice asked who was there.

"Brent Borden."

The lock released with a click and he held the door for her. Leslie rarely ventured into this part of town and she had never set foot in a homeless shelter. The lack of any frame of reference didn't prevent her from deciding that this one was barely fit for human habitation. Inside the front entrance, her toe caught on a loose flap of linoleum. She might have fallen if Brent hadn't caught her arm.

"Careful," he said quietly. "I'll fix that before we leave."

"Thanks," she said, grateful that he didn't let go right away. "Do you know those men?"

He looked down at her. "Some of them. I get called over here pretty regularly—there's always something that needs fixing—so I shoot the breeze with them for a few minutes. Come to think of it, you know one of them, too."

What? "I'm sure I've never—"

"You saw the old guy in the plaid shirt?"

She nodded, although to be honest she hadn't looked at any of them closely enough to notice what they were wearing.

"He used to be a janitor at the high school."

Leslie didn't tell him that she hadn't known any of the janitors. "Isn't that steady work? How could he end up here?"

"I have no idea, but it doesn't take much. My mother says a lot of people are just one paycheck away from being on the street."

How could that even be possible? "Sometimes I forget how lucky I am."

"Yeah," he said. "Me, too."

"If they live here, why are they sitting around outside?" she asked. "It's already getting hot out there."

"The shelter lets them stay overnight and gives them breakfast."

"And then they have to leave?"

"This place operates on a shoestring and there's always a shortage of volunteers. There's no way they can offer round-the-clock assistance."

"I see." And she wished she didn't.

"I know how you feel," he said. "Same way I feel every

time I come here. Let's find my mother and see if we can at least fix their immediate problem."

Might as well get it over with, she thought, somewhat bolstered by his hand on her shoulder. Colleen Borden's sudden appearance saved them the trouble of having to look for her.

Brent let go of Leslie's arm and set his toolbox on the floor. The hug he gave his mother was filled with genuine affection. "I don't think you've met Leslie," he said.

"Yes, we've met." Her voice was crisp and pleasant, but there was no mistaking the undertone of disapproval. "It's been a while."

"It's good to see you again," Leslie said, wishing she knew why the woman always sounded as though she was about to go on the offensive.

"The clothes my son gave you seem to fit."

Leslie could handle the barb about wearing hand-me-downs, but Colleen's emphasis on "my son" was loaded with subtext. If she had to guess, that subtext was "hands off."

Leslie willed herself to stay calm and not let herself be baited.

Brent stepped between them, as though he, too, sensed the tension. "Mom, why don't you show me where the flood is."

"It's in the basement, in the laundry area."

"So you said on the phone. Let's go down and take a look. Leslie will be fine on her own for a few minutes." As he steered his mother toward the stairs, he shot a questioning look over his shoulder at Leslie.

She shrugged and shook her head in response. So much for needing her help. He'd ended up being a referee instead. Still, she'd rather wait up here than go into the basement with Colleen Borden.

After they disappeared, Leslie became uncomfortably aware of her surroundings. The room inside the front door had a long counter and judging by the signs on the wall behind it, they made people check in, as if this were a hotel. A security camera was mounted in a corner near the ceiling. Was someone watching her?

Her skin started to crawl.

Through a doorway to her right, she could hear a television. The room was filled with an assortment of battered sofas and the television was suspended from the ceiling by metal brackets. The sole occupant, an elderly, white-haired woman, sat on one of the sofas. In spite of the TV being so loud, she was reading.

She looked familiar.

Leslie moved into the room.

The woman glanced at her.

"Hannah?"

The woman's broad, familiar smile swept Leslie back to her childhood. She set her book aside and slowly heaved herself to her feet. "Leslie Durrance. Is that really you?"

"Yes, it's me." Leslie rushed across the room and embraced the only person who had given her childhood a sense of normalcy. "Do you work here?"

"Heavens, no. I'm too old to be any good to anyone anymore, but I guess you could say I live here. I've only been here since Friday, and I hope it's temporary."

Hannah Greene, the Durrance family housekeeper for more than thirty years, was homeless? Leslie tried to remember the last time she'd seen her. "It's been too long. I think I came home after my second year at college and you weren't there. My mother said you had retired."

The elderly woman sat down again and patted the sofa. "That's right, but let's talk about you. What are you doing here, child? I know you're not homeless." The sound of her laughter made Leslie feel as though they were sitting in the Durrance kitchen. It had been Hannah's kitchen, really, and it had been the only part of Leslie's house that had felt like a home.

Leslie sat next to her. "I came here with a…a friend. He's

fixing a flooding problem in the basement." She couldn't believe how much Hannah had aged. Her shoulders were bent and she had none of the robustness that Leslie remembered so well. And she was in a homeless shelter. How could this be?

"You must be talking about Colleen's son. The two of you are still friends?"

"Oh, well, he and my brother, Nick, have been friends for years. Brent and I are just—" How could she explain why they were together on a Sunday morning if they didn't know each other? "Yes, we're still friends."

"He's a fine young man," Hannah said. "You could do worse."

Trust me, I have.

"Now tell me about yourself." Hannah took Leslie's left hand in hers. "Still not married, I see."

"No, not yet. I was engaged but we…changed our minds."

"Who broke whose heart?"

"No broken hearts," she said. "It just didn't work out." And that was the truth. It had only been twenty-four hours since she'd found out Gerald and one of her best friends were having an affair. She was mad as hell about it, but her heart was surprisingly intact.

"And you and Brent, that's working out?"

"Oh, no, it's not like that. We're just friends."

"Honey, even at my age it's easy to see he's not the kind of man a woman wants to be 'just friends' with." Hannah might be white-haired and fragile, but the same spark still brightened those gorgeous blue eyes of hers.

Leslie laughed. "There's nothing wrong with your vision, is there? You haven't told me what happened, how you ended up here."

"It's not important." She patted the book—a Bible with a frayed black cover—that lay on the sofa beside her. "I'm in good hands. Now I want to hear more about you. How's your family?"

"My brother owns a construction company. Actually, Brent works for him. And my mother is the same as ever."

"I imagined she would be," Hannah said, somewhat cryptically. "And what about you? I'll bet you did well in school."

"I did." She leaned closer and took Hannah's hand in both of hers. It felt unbelievably frail. "I went to Harvard Law School, just like you always said I would."

The old woman smiled broadly. "Another lawyer in the Durrance family. Your father would have been proud."

"I've joined his old law firm so, yes, I think he would have been pleased."

"And you're happy?"

Leslie hesitated. Two days ago she'd thought everything— her career, her husband-to-be, her future—was perfect. Since Gerald had been a mistake, she didn't feel sure about anything. "I have a good life," she said. She looked around at the peeling paint and tattered furniture. "Sometimes I forget how good."

"You've always been a sensible, hardworking girl. You deserve good things."

"So do you," she said to Hannah without hesitation.

Some throat-clearing from the doorway made them both turn around. "I see you've met Hannah," Colleen said.

"I have. We've been friends for a very long time."

"Have you?"

There was a hint of accusation in her voice, and Leslie wondered if Colleen was implying that she should have done more for Hannah. "Did Brent say how long the repairs would take?" she asked, deciding she would not let the woman get to her.

"You just got here and you already want to leave?"

Hannah squeezed her hand.

"Not at all," Leslie said, as sweetly as she could. "I was hoping to spend more time with Hannah."

"He said he'll be ten or fifteen minutes. One of the washing machines has a leaky hose, so it wasn't too serious after all." After delivering that information, Colleen about-faced and left the room.

"Thank you," Leslie called after her.

"What was that about?" Hannah asked.

"I wish I knew. When I came back to Collingwood Station to join the law firm, Colleen and I sat on a local committee for a while. She decided she didn't like me, but I've never understood why."

"Maybe it didn't have anything to do with the committee," Hannah suggested.

"Then I don't know what it could have been. We'd never met before that."

"Sometimes people make up their minds about other people before they ever have a chance to meet them."

"What do you mean?"

"It's not my place to say what Colleen Borden might have thought of you before now, but I have a feeling that if you and her son are finally going to be friends, she'll come around."

Leslie gazed into Hannah's familiar eyes and realized how much she'd missed having her, and her common-sense wisdom, in her life. "It's *so* good to see you again," she said. "There must be something I can do—"

Brent walked in, toolbox in hand. "Here you are. I wondered what you were up to."

"Finished already?" Leslie asked. "Your mother thought it might take longer."

"It was one of the less challenging plumbing problems I've had to deal with lately."

Very funny. "Do you remember Hannah Greene?"

The look he gave Hannah held no sign of recognition. "No-o-o, but I take it we've met?"

His question had Hannah chuckling. "I used to feed milk and cookies to you and Nick. You boys were quite a handful in those days."

"Of course!" He stepped forward and offered his hand. "You used to work for Leslie's family. Nice to see you again."

"Hannah hasn't told me why she's here, but it's wonderful that we've had a chance to reconnect."

"It's a blessing," Hannah said.

"Are you ready to leave?" Brent asked.

Leslie nodded at him and gave Hannah a hug. "I feel as though as I shouldn't leave you here." But given that she was temporarily homeless herself, albeit by choice, what could she do? "Will it be all right if I come back to see you?"

"I'm not going anywhere."

"Then I'll see you soon," Leslie promised. And she meant it.

"What do the two of you have planned for the rest of the day?" Hannah asked.

Leslie and Brent exchanged a quick glance. "Nothing." If one or the other had said it, it might have been convincing. Because they said it in unison, they sounded like a pair of guilty teenagers.

Hannah's smile confirmed it. "You two run along, then, and have fun doing nothing. I'm going to sit here and do a whole lot of nothing myself."

Leslie followed Brent back to the entrance. She would have been happy to slip out before his mother caught up with them, but no such luck.

"Is everything okay?" Colleen asked.

"Good as new. Well, as good as it was before the hose on one of the washing machines started leaking. I'd say they're both on their last spin cycle. Have you thought about replacing them?"

His mother gave him a you've-got-to-be-kidding-me look. "I'll just run out back and grab some cash off the money tree."

Is she always this sarcastic? Leslie wondered. *Or is there something about me that brings out the worst in her?*

"We should be going," Brent said.

"What do you have planned for the rest of the day?" his mother asked.

Leslie caught Brent's glance. That seemed to be the question of the hour.

"I guess we're going back to my place," he said.

She wished there was some way to ask his mother to keep this visit to herself, but she didn't dare.

Colleen Borden looked from one to the other, then sighed. "Have a nice day, then. Thanks for fixing the washer."

"No problem. Ready to go?" he asked Leslie.

She really wanted to get out of that place, but she also wanted to know more about Hannah's situation. "Yes, but I was wondering about Hannah," she said, lowering her voice. "Why is she here?"

"Because she has no place to live?" Colleen's quick reply was posed as a question, but it sounded more like an accusation.

And how is that my fault? Leslie took in a deep breath and told herself to stay calm. "If there's some way I can help—"

"Have you tried throwing yourself in front of the wrecking ball at that old rooming house over on Railway Avenue?"

"Mom!"

Colleen shrugged off her son's interjection. "That's where Hannah was living until she was evicted last week, along with about a dozen other people. She couldn't find anything else she could afford and with no family to help her out, she ended up here."

"I see," Leslie said. She felt physically sick. She didn't know what else to say to Brent's mother, but her thoughts were racing. For years, Hannah had been part of *her* family. Why hadn't she come to them for help? But the instant she pictured Hannah knocking on her mother's door, she had her answer. As soon as Leslie had her own life back together, she'd figure out some way to help Hannah.

Brent seemed to decide the conversation had gone on long enough. "I need to nail down that loose linoleum, then we should go."

LESLIE DIDN'T SAY any more until they were back in his truck. "Your mother really doesn't like me."

He pulled out of the parking space, then glanced at her. "Do the two of you already know each other?"

"I was on the redevelopment committee two years ago, when I first moved back to Collingwood Station. She didn't like me then, and it's pretty obvious she doesn't like me now."

"Are you still on the committee?"

"No, it was a temporary position. I was filling in for the senior partner of my father's law firm. He was working on a huge case and didn't have time for committee work."

"How long were you on the committee?"

"Six months. It was a lot more work than I'd anticipated, and almost every member seemed to have a personal agenda."

"Including my mother."

Now there was an understatement. "Especially your mother. I spent most of my time being a mediator. Collingwood Station is a small town, but it seemed to me that everyone had a huge agenda."

"Unless you were dead set against any redevelopment of any kind, you were the opposition as far as my mother was concerned. She takes that committee *very* seriously."

"No kidding. She treats everyone like an adversary."

He gave her a sharp sideways glance.

"I'm sorry, but it's true."

"Trust me, I can quote all my mother's reasons, chapter and

verse, for why redevelopment should stop. But I make my living by turning some of those rundown properties into showpieces. Don't think she isn't on my case from time to time."

"That must be awkward."

"My mother's heart is in the right place. It's her mission in life to help those less fortunate than she is. I guess it's a good thing she isn't all that well off, so those less fortunate make up a relatively small group. I do what I can to help out around the shelter and that seems to appease her."

Leslie didn't know what she could do to help the shelter but she could do something for Hannah. And she would. "Do you know what's being built to replace Hannah's old building on Railway Avenue?" she asked.

"Condos."

"I see." Did Brent's mother think Leslie had something to do with that? The woman was so unreasonable that her opinions weren't worth losing sleep over, but Leslie hated it when people judged her. Or, in the case of Colleen Borden, *mis*judged her.

Brent pulled into the driveway and turned off the engine. Then he covered her hand with his. "Give her a chance, okay? She'll come around."

He sounded so certain that she didn't have the heart to disagree. Besides, did it really matter? She and Brent would go their separate ways when she went home and it wouldn't matter what Colleen thought of her.

Brent made no move to get out of the truck. Leslie glanced at him then averted her gaze, suddenly feeling awkward. Was he reluctant to go inside? Was he wondering the same thing she was? What were they going to do for the rest of the day?

"Your house has so much character. How long have you lived here?"

"Three years, although the first two were more like camping. The place needed a lot work, but I think it was worth it." He finally opened his door.

Remembering how he'd carried her to the front door yesterday, Leslie quickly opened hers and climbed out before he had a chance to help.

Brent slammed his door and paused. "That's weird," he said.

"What?"

"Max isn't barking. I wonder what he's up to."

"Maybe he's sleeping."

"He'd have woken up the second he heard us pull into the yard."

"Do you think he's okay?"

"Yeah, but I hope he hasn't destroyed anything."

Chapter Seven

After Brent unlocked the door, Leslie followed him inside, hoping Max was all right. And that he hadn't found her teddy bear on the nightstand.

"Max?" Brent called. "Oh, no." He bent down and picked up her wedding shoes.

Her very badly chewed wedding shoes.

"Max!" he yelled. "Where are you?"

"Please don't worry about this," she said. "I shouldn't have left them here."

"They're ruined."

That was true. Several of the thin straps had been completely chewed through. There were teeth marks in the heels, and the end of one had been gnawed off.

Brent handed the shoes to her and went in search of Max. They found him in Brent's bedroom, hiding under the bed. Rather, he'd stuck his head under the bed frame. The rest of him was out in the open and his back end was aimed toward the doorway.

Leslie laughed, but Brent was clearly not amused. "Max, come out of there."

She put a hand on his arm. "Don't yell at him. It's not his fault."

"I'm really sorry about this. I'll pay for them."

"You don't have to do that." Besides, she'd be too embarrassed to tell him how much they cost. "I'll never wear them again."

"I'll say." Brent pointed to a severed ankle strap. "There's no way these can be repaired."

"I wouldn't have worn them again even if this hadn't happened. They were only going to end up in the back of my closet."

He gave her an odd smile. "Well, at least they were too big to fit down the drain."

"What's that supposed to mean?"

"I was kidding."

"Ha, ha."

"You're awfully blasé about all this stuff."

"I'm not 'blasé' about anything. These things are all about the wedding that wasn't. I don't need those kinds of reminders, and FYI, Mr. Borden, I will not apologize for having money. It's bad enough that your mother thinks it's a fatal flaw, but I didn't expect it from you."

He ran a hand across his face. "I was out of line, and I'm sorry. But I *will* replace the shoes."

"Please don't. I don't want another pair."

Max was still in self-imposed exile. She set the shoes on the bed, trying not to be distracted by the tousled sheets and the dent in Brent's pillow, and knelt beside the dog. "Does he really think he's hiding?"

"He can't see us, so he thinks we can't see him."

The dog's head appeared as soon as she touched him, but he kept it low, gazing sheepishly at her through his bangs. "Poor Max. You feel badly about this, don't you?" She glanced over her shoulder at Brent. "I think he's trying to apologize."

"He always seems to know when he's done something wrong but for some reason he can't figure that out until after he's done it."

"We all make mistakes." Leslie put her arms around the dog's neck. "It's okay, Max. No one's mad at you." She stole another look at Brent. "Right?"

"I'd better take him for a w-a-l-k and let him run off some steam."

"Why are you spelling *walk?*"

Max perked up and stared at her for a few seconds before tearing out of the room.

She stood up, laughing. "He knows what that means?"

"He's gone to get his leash. Come and see for yourself."

She followed him into the kitchen in time to see Max pull his leash off a hook by the French doors. "Wow, that's pretty smart."

"Bring it here, boy." Max dropped the leash into Brent's outstretched hand. "He also knows c-a-r, b-a-l-l and r-a-b-b-i-t," he said as he clipped the leash to the dog's collar.

"Rabbit?"

That word sent Max into another frenzy. He raced to the door, dragging his leash behind him and nearly knocking Leslie over in the process. His ears stood at attention, then he started barking wildly as he scanned the backyard.

"That's why you have to spell it. Come on, Max. Let's go." Brent crossed the room and grabbed the leash. "We'll be back in half an hour. Or you could come with us."

"Thanks, but I think I'll stay here." If she could run into someone she knew at the homeless shelter, anyone might see them together at the park. There was going to be plenty of gossip and she didn't want to drag Brent into it. "If it's okay with you, I'll decide what to make for dinner tonight and breakfast tomorrow."

"Unless it's macaroni minus the cheese with maybe a side of ketchup, I'd say we're out of luck."

"Then I'll make a shopping list and you can go to the grocery store when you get back." It sounded more domestic than she'd intended, and she hoped he didn't notice.

"You don't have to cook." But he sounded hopeful.

"I don't mind." And part of her wanted him to be impressed that she was a very good cook.

Max pulled him toward the front door. "Gotta go. There's a notepad stuck to the fridge," he said before he disappeared.

She watched them from the living room window and when they reached the end of the block, she returned to the kitchen and dialed in to her voice mail.

Eight more messages. "Why can't you people leave me alone?"

She deleted them as she listened. Allison; her mother; two more from Allison, who had sent her poor husband to the town house again that morning; a neighbor who wondered if everything was okay; one of the partners from the law firm; and a reporter from the local paper.

She pictured herself going home and fighting her way through a crush of microphones and flashbulbs. "You're being ridiculous," she said to herself. "It probably has something to do with one of the cases you're working on."

But was she ready to go home and find out? No.

The last call was from Gerald, and this time he'd left a message. "We need to talk, Leslie. This was all just a misunderstanding."

Sure it was, Gerald. Exactly which part of you feeling up one of my bridesmaids did I misunderstand?

She tore a sheet off the notepad on the fridge and sat down to make a grocery list. Brent had been right. What was the point of listening to messages when all they did was make her furious with everyone, including her family and her best friend?

After a quick inventory of Brent's cupboards, she sat down and listed everything she needed to make dinner. She was adding the ingredients for French toast when Brent and Max returned. Brent unfastened the dog's leash and put it back on its hook. Max headed for his water bowl for a drink.

"He seems much calmer," Leslie said. Surprisingly, so was she.

"That was the plan," Brent said.

Sure enough, Max wandered from his water bowl to the living room where he flopped onto a big green-and-maroon-plaid cushion in front of the fireplace and closed his eyes.

Brent picked up the list and scanned it. "What's fennel?"

"It's a vegetable. A white bulb…" She indicated the size with her hands. "With long, feathery green stems."

He looked puzzled. "Never heard of it."

"It tastes like licorice."

"Ah, they say licorice is an aphrodisiac."

Her face went warm. "Well, this isn't licorice. It only tastes like it."

"Works for me." There was a sexy promise in his smile.

"I'm making pasta sauce, not oysters Rockefeller."

"But it's licorice pasta sauce."

"It's fennel-infused marinara sauce."

"Interesting."

"It's delicious."

"I'm sure it is," he said, eyes still filled with mischief.

"But fennel is not…"

He leaned close, within kissing distance, and her breath caught in her throat. Before she had a chance to react, he planted a kiss on top of her head. "I'll be back as quick as I can."

She heard the front door close, and then his truck as it backed out of the driveway. "By the way, fennel is not an aphrodisiac." Still, putting up with Brent's occasional nonsense was infinitely easier than having to cope with everyone else in her life.

BRENT MANEUVERED his shopping cart up and down the aisles of the grocery store, scanning the shelves for the things on Leslie's list. The place was crazy busy, which seemed strange for a Sunday afternoon.

He wedged the cart between one that was equipped with a baby seat, complete with a sleeping baby, and a stock boy with a trolley-load of canned mushrooms. Canned tomatoes had to be around here someplace.

"Help you find something?" the stock boy asked.

Brent watched, mildly amused, as the kid tossed each can and caught it before sliding it onto the shelf. That explained why so many cans ended up with dents in them.

"I need a large can of Italian tomatoes."

"Sure thing. They're halfway up the aisle on your left."

"Thanks." He tried to swing back into traffic and bumped the cart next to him. The baby's mouth made little sucking motions but its eyes—her eyes, judging by the pink outfit—remained closed. "Sorry," he said.

The young mother glared at him and then cut him off before he could get rolling.

Man, this place was worse than rush hour on the freeway.

When he finally found the tomatoes, he tossed two cans into the cart.

He double-checked the list. He had everything but the fresh vegetables, so he headed for the produce department. Along the way he grabbed a family-sized box of corn flakes and a half dozen packages of mac and cheese. After all, he'd have to feed himself once Leslie was gone.

The produce section was as insane as the rest of the store but thanks to her accurate description of the fennel, he found it right away. And it did smell like licorice. Her indignant reaction to his calling it an aphrodisiac had made this whole shopping trip worthwhile, and he imagined he could get even more mileage out of that once they were having dinner. Now all he needed were the fresh basil, onions and—

"Hey, Brent. How's it going?" Nick asked, giving him a friendly slap on the shoulder.

Damn. His best friend, aka Leslie's brother, was the last person he needed to see right now. "Good. How 'bout you?"

"Good. Maggie sent me here to pick up a few things," he said.

"I see."

Nick scanned the contents of Brent's cart and then focused on the list in his hand. "Since I know you well enough to know you don't make lists, or cook, I'm guessing somebody sent you here, too."

"Right, yeah, we're just doing some kind of pasta thing for dinner."

"The message you left yesterday said you were going out of town for a few days."

"Oh, that. We, ah, changed our minds. Decided to stay in town instead."

"I see. So you'll be at work tomorrow?"

"Yeah, sure. No problem."

Nick picked up the fennel and studied it. "I didn't know you were seeing anyone."

"Right, well, I didn't want to say anything, you know, in case it didn't work out."

Nick put the weird-looking vegetable back in the cart. "I guess there's a first time for everything."

It dawned on Brent that he could have said he was shopping for his mother, but it was too late. He'd blown that one.

"So," Nick said. "Are you going to ask how the wedding went yesterday?"

"Oh, right. How was it?" But he was sure he looked as guilty as a bank robber caught with a wad of cash.

"I guess you haven't heard, then." Nick was clearly baiting him.

Brent responded with a casual shrug. "Heard what?"

Nick was eyeing him suspiciously. "Leslie didn't go through with it."

"You don't say?"

"Strangest thing, too. She took off and no one knows where she is."

"Humph."

"Well, I should get going. Maggie's waiting at home for this stuff." He started to walk away, then stopped. "By the way, I was talking to John Fontaine this morning. He said he ran into you over at the pharmacy yesterday."

Busted, Brent thought. Still, he wasn't going to be the one to blow Leslie's cover. "I forgot about that. I didn't have a chance to talk to him, though."

"Really?"

"Yeah, you know how it is. I never had much in common with that guy."

"True. So I guess I'll see you tomorrow morning."

"Bright and early." He watched Nick walk in the direction of the cashiers and waited till he was out of sight before he looked at the list again.

What else did he need?

Basil, onions and garlic.

He added them to the cart and killed five minutes by pretending to look at the rest of the produce section. There was some weird stuff here, and he'd bet Leslie knew how to cook all of it. When he finally pushed the cart to the checkout area and surveyed the crowd, there was no sign of Nick.

After he paid for the groceries and loaded them in his truck, he dropped into a wine shop and asked the owner to recommend something to go with Leslie's marinara sauce. He was tempted to stop at the florist next door and buy her a pink rose, but he stopped himself.

This wasn't a date and if he tried to move too fast, he'd never have a chance. For tonight he'd have to rely on his charm—and the licorice-flavored pasta sauce.

AFTER DINNER Leslie watched Brent turn on the tap and squirt a stream of soap into the sink. "Thanks for cooking," he said. "That was a great dinner."

She carried their plates and cutlery across the kitchen and set them on the counter next to the sink. "You're welcome. I'm glad you liked it."

"Hannah's influence, right?" He picked up the stack of dishes and slid them into the sink.

She reached for a towel. "It was, and as soon as my life is back to normal, I'm going to help her get back on her feet."

He took the towel away from her. "No way. The cook never cleans."

"When people share a meal, I always think that cleaning up together is kind of—" Intimate. She couldn't believe she'd almost said that. The way Brent had looked at her throughout the meal suggested he didn't need any encouragement. "It just seems like the right thing to do."

He conceded and gave the towel back. "What do you have in mind for Hannah?"

"Finding her a decent place to live."

"You heard what my mother said. There isn't a lot of affordable housing in town. Practically none."

"Hannah might not be able to afford it, but I can."

He rinsed a plate and stood it in the rack. "You'd do that for her?"

"She was practically my second mother." Or she would have been, if Leslie's own mother had ever seemed like the first. "I used to spend hours in the kitchen with her. That was my first introduction to cooking."

"So that's why I never saw much of you when I was hanging out with Nick."

She shrugged. She had always made herself scarce when Brent was there because she had never been able to figure out how to handle his constant flirting. "My parents were busy, and Nick was into sports and spending time with his friends, but Hannah didn't seem to mind having me around."

"It always seemed like you had everything you ever wanted," he said.

"Money isn't everything. If I ever have children, they won't spend most of their time with the housekeeper."

He tweaked the end of her nose with a sudsy finger, leaving a blob of bubbles behind. "I'm sorry. I just never imagined that's how things were for you. Nick never let on—"

She scrunched her nose and wiped the soap away, flicking it at Brent. She couldn't believe she'd let down her guard. She had never confessed to anyone that her childhood had been lonely. Not to any of her friends, not to Gerald, not even to her own family. Why now? Why Brent?

"Nick was always better at ignoring those things than I was, but I survived."

"Money might not be everything," he said, "but if it'll help you get Hannah out of the shelter, that's more than a lot of people could do."

"It's not a big deal." She smiled as she dried the last glass and set it on the counter, then used the towel to wipe the suds from his hair and forehead.

She thought he might smile back, but he didn't. Instead, his stare was intense, and she suddenly had trouble breathing.

He recovered first. "Well, looks like we're done here. There's a ball game on. Do you mind if I turn on the TV?"

"Of course not. Who's playing?"

"The Yankees and Boston."

"I've always been a Red Sox fan."

"Since when have you been into baseball?"

"I went to a few games when I was at university."

"Being a fan involves more than going to a few games. Take the Yankees, for example. Now there's a team."

She followed him into the living room.

Brent picked up a remote off the top of a corner cabinet, opened the doors, and turned on the TV.

Max was curled up on one end of the sofa. Brent sat at the other end and Leslie had no choice but to sit between them.

"All right. Bottom of the third, still no runs."

Leslie leaned forward and looked at the coffee table. It had a recessed top that was filled with baseball memorabilia and covered with glass.

"Did you build this table?" she asked.

"I did," he said, without taking his eyes off the screen.

The table contained a collection of baseball cards, a battered glove that bore a signature she couldn't make out and a couple of autographed balls. Interesting.

"Back in high school, weren't you the star player on the team?" she asked, although she already knew the answer to that question. There had even been talk of him going to college on a full scholarship.

"You could say that."

"But you didn't pursue it?"

He tore his gaze away from the TV long enough to answer her question. "I gave it a shot but college wasn't for me. And it was a lot easier being a big fish in a small pond."

"Do you miss it?"

He seemed to give that some consideration before he answered. "No, I don't. Playing ball was fun, but the work I do suits me better."

And you're a master at it, she thought, running a hand along the edge of the table. She wondered how he'd happened upon this as a career when playing baseball had seemed like such a sure thing. Her Life List, which was starting to feel more like a dark tunnel than a route map for her life, hadn't had that kind of flexibility. She had never considered the possibility of not going into law, and she wondered now what she might have done if circumstances had been different. Would she be happier than she was now? She certainly would have had more fun in school.

The game caught his attention and she turned hers back to the table. There was a photograph of the high school team, taken at her place, the day they'd won the state championship. Nick had been the team's shortstop, and he'd hosted the party.

Brent used to hang out at her place with her brother and they had been easy enough to avoid until Nick had started dating Allison. When it was just the guys, Leslie would make herself scarce. When Allison was there, it was harder to stay out of sight, so Leslie usually invited other people over, as well. Anyone would do, as long as it meant she and Brent and Allison and Nick weren't a foursome.

That spring she and Allison had gone shopping in the city and they'd bought the skimpiest bikinis they could find. Correction. That Allison could find. They were meant to be worn by girls with a *Baywatch* figure like Allison's, not underdeveloped sixteen-year-olds, but Leslie had let herself be talked into it. She'd also let herself be talked into wearing it at that pool party, and it had attracted way more attention than she'd wanted.

Brent glanced at her. "What are you looking at?"

"The picture taken at the pool party."

Brent laughed. "Nick was the worst shortstop in the history of baseball. We only kept him on the team because he threw the best parties."

As she recalled, it was one of the worst parties she'd ever been to.

"Something wrong?" he asked.

"No, I was just remembering something."

"Something unpleasant, if I had to guess." He shifted sideways and put an arm across the back of the sofa. The game on TV was forgotten and his full attention was focused on her.

"It was nothing, and I was just a silly teenager in those days."

He was studying her closely now. "Didn't you get upset about something?"

Leslie was starting to feel as self-conscious as she had back in those days. She looked down at her hands and wished she'd never mentioned the party.

"Was it something I did?"

"Sort of."

"Then you might as well get it off your chest. You may never get the chance again."

"It's not like I've been holding a grudge." Although that was not entirely true.

"Spill it," was all he said.

She knew he wouldn't drop the subject, and she had never been good at making up stories. "A week or so before the party Allison and I were shopping and she talked me into a buying a new bathing suit."

Brent's eyes lit up. "Ah, the pink bikini."

"You remember?"

"Not an easy thing to forget."

Heat flamed across her face. "I got a bit of a sunburn that day."

"Like you have now?" he asked.

"This isn't from too much sun."

He stroked the tip of his index finger the length of her nose. "I know."

She brushed his hand away. "Someone told me my nose was getting pink and that I should put on some sunscreen, and you said—"

She couldn't say it.

"And I said…what?"

"And you said, 'A little bit of pink can be kind of nice.'"

"Oh-kay." But it was obvious that he didn't understand what she was saying.

"When you said it, you weren't looking at my nose."

He blinked, apparently still not following. "So what was

I…" Then his slow-spreading grin let her know that he got it. "Right."

"It wasn't funny."

"Come on, Leslie. What was I, sixteen? Seventeen? Guys that age are morons. They always look at girls that way."

She wanted to point out that using ignorance as a defense never worked on a lawyer, but he'd probably find that funny, too. "It wasn't that you were looking at me, it was what you said. In front of everyone."

He was back to looking confused. "What was it I said again?"

"That a *little bit* of pink was nice."

He closed his eyes for a few seconds then shook his head. To her satisfaction, a few traces of pink had found a home on his face, too. "And you thought I meant—"

"Exactly what you said." What else was she supposed to think? The other girls were spilling out of their swimsuits, only too happy to be ogled, while she'd had nothing to spill. Still didn't.

"I don't remember saying it but if it'll make you feel any better, I can tell you exactly what I was thinking."

She looked away. Under the present circumstances, that might not be such a good idea.

He seemed to think otherwise. He hooked a finger under her chin and turned her head until their gazes met. Then he slowly, and very deliberately, lowered his eyes until they settled on her breasts. "I would have been thinking the same thing I'm thinking right now. That you are gorgeous and sexy and if you're going to wear a bikini, you'd better get used to guys looking at you."

Just as slowly, his gaze made the return trip, and she hoped he'd looked away before her nipples had gone hard. She tried to inch away from him and ended up bumping into Max. The dog sat up, apparently annoyed that his nap had been disturbed, jumped off the sofa, and settled himself on the big green-and-maroon-plaid cushion by the fireplace.

Brent closed the small space she'd managed to open between them and put his hands on her shoulders. "Would you like me to show you what I really wanted to do that day?"

The breathless anticipation of his kiss prevented her from her talking, so she simply shook her head.

"Was that a no?"

She nodded.

"That looked more like a yes."

Probably because it was.

Chapter Eight

That kiss was everything last night's wasn't—demanding, possessive, deeply intimate. His hands were everywhere, and they were just as skilled at making love as they were at everything else he did. Stroking her hair, testing the soft part of her earlobe before his mouth explored it further.

Somehow she'd gone from sitting to lying beneath him, and he was nudging her legs apart with one knee. The anticipation was almost more than she could stand.

And then his mouth was back on hers and his tongue sparked off even more exquisite sensations. One hand worked its way down her rib cage and found the hem of her shirt. His hand hesitated, and she tried to predict which direction it would take. Up or down? Either would work. It just needed to move faster.

When it inched its way upward, she realized she'd been hoping for the opposite. Then her nipple was being rolled between his fingers and direction no longer mattered because every part of her hummed with pleasure.

Her own hands crawled under his shirt and up his back.

She arched against him, no longer able to resist touching him the way he touched her.

"Slow down."

"No," she said. All her life she'd taken things slow. Tonight she was in the mood for a little speed.

"I can't believe this is happening." That brought her back to reality, or at least the outskirts.

She couldn't believe it, either. Her chest heaved as she tried to breathe. Yesterday she'd been on her way to the altar to marry one man and now she was breathing heavily with another. And not just *any* other guy. Brent had always made it clear he was interested in her. Leading him on like this wasn't right.

He raised his head and looked down at her. "You don't want to do this, do you?"

She let out a long breath. "The outside me does. The inside me isn't so sure it's a good idea."

He sighed softly. "For now I think we'd better listen to the inside you."

She still clung to him.

He pulled his hand from under her shirt and moved away. "I hope the inside you changes her mind someday." He kissed her again, lightly, and she knew it would be the last until she made a decision.

Another few minutes of that hand under her shirt might have tipped the balance. She grasped his wrist and tried to indicate that, but he gently moved her hand and helped her to sit up.

"I've waited a long time for this. It won't kill me to wait until you know what you want."

"What if I never figure that out?"

"Then I'm seriously going to regret that I stopped."

So will I, Leslie thought. "Can we still watch the ball game together?"

"That we can do." He paused, then held out an arm for her. "Come here."

In spite of what had just happened, or maybe because of it, curling up in the protective circle of his arm seemed like the natural thing to do. She settled in and closed her eyes. "What's happening with the game?"

"Top of the fourth," he said. "Yankees are up by two."

"The Red Sox will even the score."

"We'll see about that." He smoothed the hair on her fore-head and she could tell he was looking at her. "I'm really sorry, Leslie. There must've been times when I acted like a jerk, but I never meant to hurt you."

She opened her eyes and smiled up at him. "I know."

LESLIE TOSSED and turned most of the night. The room wasn't equipped with a clock of any kind and she didn't have a wrist-watch with her, so she didn't know exactly when she'd reached a decision. Once she had, she'd slept fitfully for maybe an hour or two. At the crack of dawn she quietly crawled out of bed and slipped into her jeans and a light-blue T-shirt that Brent had given her.

Max was at her door. "Shh," she whispered. "I don't want to wake Brent."

The clock in the kitchen said it was just before six. She hated to wake Nick, but she wanted to ask him to pick her up this morning, and she needed to talk to him before Brent got up and tried to change her mind.

After four rings, a groggy but familiar voice came on the line. "Hello?"

"Nick? It's me, Leslie."

"Hey, what time is it?"

"Quarter to six."

"That explains why I'm not awake."

"I'm ready to go home. I was hoping you wouldn't mind picking me up this morning."

"No problem. Where are you?"

"I'm at Brent's place."

Silence.

"Nick?"

"Yeah, I'm still here. Surprised, though."

Oddly enough, he didn't sound all that surprised. "It's a

long story. I can explain everything later, but if you wouldn't mind picking me up, maybe on your way to work, that would be great."

"Are you okay?"

"I'm fine, but I can't stay here forever."

"True."

"Can you do a favor for me? Allison has left about a dozen messages for me and in one of them she said she has my handbag with the keys to my town house. Can you get it from her before you pick me up?"

"Sure. I'll be there around nine. Will that work?"

"That's perfect. You won't tell Allison where I am, will you?"

"Won't say a thing."

She was tempted to ask about their mother, but that could wait. "Nick?"

"Yeah?"

"Thanks."

"No problem."

After she hung up, she walked over to the French doors and looked out at the backyard. Max scratched lightly at the door, so she unlocked it and let him out, hoping he wouldn't start barking.

She opened the fridge and took out the milk, butter and a carton of eggs, and nudged the door shut with her foot. She turned around and there was Brent, standing on the other side of the room.

"Good morning," he said. "Sleep well?"

"Not particularly."

"Me, neither."

She unloaded her armful of dairy products onto the counter. "I wanted to get up early and make that French toast I promised you."

"Don't worry about it." The coolness in his voice told her that he had heard her on the phone with her brother.

"Brent, it's time for me to go home," she said. "Nick is coming to pick me up."

"You didn't have to call him. I would have taken you."

"I know, but first you would have tried to talk me out of it."

"That's true. I would have. If this is about last night—"

"It isn't."

He clearly didn't believe her, and rightly so. It had everything to do with last night.

"Let me qualify that," she said. "It's not completely about last night. I can't hide forever. My family's worried about me and they need to know I'm okay."

"Do you plan to go back to work right away?"

"No, I arranged to take several weeks off and I'd like to take advantage of the time to do a few things, like rescue Hannah from the shelter." She looked down at the floor while she searched for the right words. "I also have to get Gerald out of my life for good, and the only way to do that is to confront him."

Brent looked defeated. "You know what he's going to say, don't you? That he's sorry and he wants you back."

Did he really think she'd be tempted by anything Gerald could possibly say? "I don't know what to expect, but this is something I have to do. He and I are over. I don't have room in my life for a man who cheats on me, and there's nothing he can say to make me change my mind. But I can't move forward—either on my own or with someone else—until I've ended this with him."

"So when you say 'someone else,' does that mean—"

"No, Brent. It's too soon for that. But I'm glad you found me on Saturday and brought me here. I needed a friend, and you were there." She moved toward him and he opened his arms for her. Learning to lean on this man and his quiet strength would be dangerously easy.

"I need to confess something," he said.

She tipped her head back and looked up at him. "What is it?"

He ran his hand up her neck and over the back of her head, gently bringing her cheek to rest on his chest. "My being there on Saturday morning wasn't a coincidence."

She tried to look up again, but he wouldn't let her. "If it wasn't a coincidence, then what was it?" she asked.

"Nick told me you were getting married. I guess I needed to know if it was really happening."

She swung her head up to face him and that time he didn't try to stop her. "I had no idea it would have mattered to you."

"Neither did I. And then there I was, driving past the church."

"And there I was, running down the sidewalk in the pouring rain. I must have looked like a lunatic."

"It was...unexpected."

"Of all the people who could have found me, I'm glad it was you."

His arms tightened around her.

"Brent, that still doesn't mean—"

"I know," he said. "I get it. But I wanted you to know why I was there."

"Thank you. And we're going to be friends, right?" She held her breath and waited.

He didn't answer right away. "For sure," he said finally.

Moving away from him wasn't easy, but she finally backed out of his arms. "I should get started on breakfast."

"Can I help?"

"You already have."

Brent mopped up the maple syrup on his plate with the last piece of French toast. He could get used to eating like this. He was already used to having Leslie here and he didn't want to think about how the house would feel after she left. "This is really good. What's your secret?"

"Cinnamon, although I wouldn't call it a secret."

"Well, it's the best I've ever tasted. Just don't tell my mother I said that."

"Are you kidding? I'm already her least favorite person."

"I wouldn't say that," he said, wishing he hadn't brought up the subject. "So, I guess you're looking forward to being back in your own place."

"Yes, but I'll miss being here. You have a wonderful home."

"The door is always open." As if to demonstrate the point, Max ambled in through the open French doors and made a beeline for Leslie. Brent watched the dog put his head on her lap and get rewarded with a pat on the head.

"I'm going to miss Max, too. Maybe I can take him for a wa—" She caught herself before she said the word. "A w-a-l-k sometime."

He thought that was an odd thing for her to offer until she indicated the notepad on the fridge. "I noticed you have a dog walker. Mandi? If there are times when she's not available, I'd be happy to come over and take him out."

If he didn't know better, he'd suspect she was looking for an excuse to come back. "Sure," he said. "Mandi's the teenager across the street. She's always been reliable but that could change now that she has a driver's license."

Was she serious about walking Max, he wondered, or had she just been fishing to find out about Mandi? Either way, he was happy to clear up any confusion about the relationship he and Max had with their dog walker. He wanted her to know there were no other women in his life, and as long as he thought he had a shot with her, there wouldn't be.

She glanced up at the clock. "I should get my things together. Nick will be here soon."

"Do you need a bag or anything?"

"No, thanks. I still have the one the clothes were in."

Right. After she left the kitchen, he piled the dishes into the sink and poured himself another cup of coffee. It wasn't as strong as he usually made it, but it tasted better. He'd have to remember that.

A few minutes later he heard Nick pull into his driveway, and then the sound of footsteps on the veranda and a couple of loud knocks on the front door. This he was not looking forward to.

"Leslie?" he called on his way through the living room. "Nick's here."

She appeared with her bag in hand. "I'm ready."

He opened the door. "Hey."

"Hey." Nick looked past him to Leslie. His eyes softened immediately. "You okay?"

"I'm fine. Brent has taken good care of me."

Nick's questioning gaze was back on him, and the question was all too clear. *What the hell has been going on?*

Nothing. Everything. None of your damn business.

"Right," Nick said. "We should go. Maggie's waiting out in the truck."

Leslie glanced over his shoulder and waved. "I'm so glad she came with you."

Brent watched him take Leslie's bag. "Ready to go?" Nick asked.

She nodded. "As soon as I say goodbye to Brent."

Nick's gaze flicked from her to Brent and back again. "I can wait outside."

"You don't have to do that," she said.

To Brent's surprise, she put her arms around his neck and kissed him. Not on the mouth, but close enough that it wasn't a kiss on the cheek, either.

He knew better than to return it.

"Thank you," she said. "For everything." She looked directly into his eyes as she said it, and he struggled to understand the subtext.

Everything?

Her smile let him know she meant *everything*. "And I'm sorry about the plumbing. How a *girl* can cause that much trouble is kind of a *mystery*."

If he hadn't already known he was completely, head-over-heels back in love with her, he would have realized it then. He wanted to ask when he could see her again, but he didn't. He couldn't, not with Nick watching. "See you around."

"See you. Say goodbye to Max for me."

"Will do."

Nick stepped aside and let her go out ahead of him. "I'm not sure how long this will take," he said to Brent. "Might be a good idea to hold off and start the new job tomorrow."

"Works for me." He would rather have started today, but he should be able to find enough around his place to keep himself busy. "See you tomorrow morning."

Nick still looked as though he had a question or two, or twenty, but he didn't ask. "See you."

Brent closed the door. From the living room window, he watched them drive away. They weren't even at the end of the block and already the house felt empty.

LESLIE DIDN'T SAY much on the ride to her place. She didn't have to. Maggie kept up a steady stream of chatter about the amazing job that Nick and Brent had done of renovating her house and her excitement about opening her new business.

"This afternoon is the grand opening of Inner Beauty Spa," she said. "You're welcome to drop in."

"I'd like to, but I have a lot of things to catch up on. Can I take a rain check?"

"Of course. Call me and we'll set up an appointment for any time that works for you. It'll be my treat."

"That's so sweet, but you don't have to do that."

"Oh, I want to. You've been through a lot these last few days."

Nick's throat-clearing made Leslie laugh. Maggie's straight-forwardness was refreshing, and she was exactly the kind of person her brother needed in his life right now.

"I have been, and I appreciate everything the two of you are doing for me."

When they arrived at Leslie's town house complex, Nick pulled into the small parking area in front of her garage.

"Would the two of you like to come in for a while? To be honest, I'm not sure I'm quite ready to be alone."

They glanced at each other and after a moment of silent communication, they both nodded.

"Here's your purse," Maggie said as she passed it to her.

"Thanks." Leslie opened it and found her keys.

They all got out of the truck and Leslie unlocked her front door.

Maggie had a large paper grocery bag in her arms. "We stopped at Donaldson's Deli and picked up a few things for you. Since you were planning to be on your honeymoon, we thought you probably would have cleaned out your fridge."

For a few seconds Nick managed to pry his eyes off the love of his life and smile at Leslie. "Never would have occurred to me," he said. "Maggie gets all the credit."

"That's so thoughtful," Leslie said, but she was thinking about the way Nick looked at Maggie. Gerald had never looked at her that way, but Brent had.

"We weren't sure if you'd feel like shopping, so there's bread and cheese and eggs and fruit in there. And milk. We should probably get that in the fridge."

The town house seemed awfully quiet, almost eerily so, and Leslie was relieved she hadn't had to come home alone. She set her bag of clothes on the floor in the foyer and led the way to the kitchen.

Maggie promptly made herself at home. "You two sit and chat," she said. "I'll put these things away and make tea."

It felt great to let someone like Maggie take charge and organize things. She was so nonjudgmental, which was a rarity in this town. And Nick was as supportive as possible, given that he was definitely the strong, silent type.

"Have you talked with Mother?" she asked.

"I don't know if 'talked with her' is the way I'd describe it. She insisted I call her the minute I heard from you."

"Did you?"

"No. Must have slipped my mind."

She laughed. "Thanks. I'll call her tomorrow. Or the next day. I just need a little time."

"Now that Allison knows you've resurfaced, you might not be able to stay in hiding much longer."

"I'll call her, too. She can be more discreet than people give her credit for." Sometimes.

But the real question was, how many people knew about Gerald and Candice? She decided to choose her words carefully. "You're probably wondering what happened at the church on Saturday."

Nick and Maggie exchanged a look. "We know," her brother said. "Maggie saw them together."

"I see." If Maggie saw them, then others may have seen them, too. "Does Allison know?"

The two of them exchanged another glance.

Okay, this was not looking good. "All right, what about Mother? Did anyone tell her?"

Nick held up both hands, palms out. "Hey, if she knows anything, she didn't hear it from us."

"And what about…"

"Gerald?"

She was getting tired of hearing his name. "Has he tried to get in touch with you?"

"He wouldn't dare. As soon as I announced to everyone in the church that there wasn't going to be a wedding, he made himself scarce. I thought about paying him a visit, but I didn't want to do anything I might regret."

She remembered what Brent had said, that Nick should have said something about her choice of husbands. "Maybe you and Brent should pay him a visit together."

"Maybe we should."

Maggie set a pot of tea and three cups on the table. "You're lucky to have a brother," she said. "Someone to look out for you."

"I am, although it's taken me a long time to figure that out."

AFTER Nick and Maggie left, Leslie locked the dead bolt and slid the security chain into place. She didn't think Gerald would have the nerve to use his key, but she wasn't taking any chances. When she did see him again, it would be on her terms.

She'd meant what she'd said to Brent earlier, that she couldn't move on until she'd ended things with Gerald. Not that there was any doubt that it was already over, but it wouldn't feel final until she'd confronted him and told him so. Not that she was in any hurry to see him, but when she did, he wouldn't know what hit him.

In the den, she quickly scrolled through her call display to see who had called and decided the messages could wait. She picked up the bag she'd left by the door and took it upstairs. She dropped it on her bed and went into the bathroom. Maybe she'd feel more like herself after she'd showered and conditioned her hair. And moisturized, and put on some makeup and got dressed in her own clothes. Then she thought about Maggie's offer. Maybe she would go for a facial today.

Gerald's things were neatly organized by his sink. Except it wasn't his sink anymore, and she suddenly had a very different priority. The shower could wait.

She went back downstairs to the garage and found an empty box. On her way through the kitchen, she grabbed his favorite coffee mug out of the cupboard and dropped it in the box. In the bedroom, she hesitated. He didn't have that many clothes here, but she'd pack those after she finished in the bathroom. She set the box on the vanity, scooped up his soap and toothbrush and dumped them in. Then she yanked open his drawer and started tossing.

Dental floss, deodorant, cologne. Revolting stuff. What a relief to not have to smell that again. She had always disliked it, and yet she had never told him. Whatever Brent used suited her perfectly.

You need to focus, she told herself. Gerald needed to be fully banished from her life before she let herself think about anyone else.

It was difficult not to think about Brent, though. The time she'd spent with him had flown by, and it had been full of unexpected surprises. Maybe if the circumstances had been different…

But aside from running away from the man she'd been about to marry, what other circumstances could have landed her at Brent's place? None that she could think of.

She picked up the box, carried it into the bedroom and set it on the bed. She removed her thrift-shop clothes from the bag and unfolded the T-shirt the diamonds were wrapped in. After she retrieved the jeweler's cases from a drawer in her dresser and put the jewelry in them, she put them in the box with everything else. Carefully, but firmly. In a few minutes she had Gerald's clothes off their hangers and out of her drawers, then she hauled the box back downstairs and put it in the den.

Now she had something important to do. She went back upstairs and put away the things Brent had given her—everything but the teddy bear, which she set on the dresser. Then she headed for the shower. Half an hour later she was scrubbed, primped, dressed and ready for a little pampering.

Chapter Nine

Maggie's purple house, with its red door and white picket fence, was definitely an attention grabber. Nick and Brent had just finished renovating it, and Leslie couldn't wait to see the interior. She glanced cautiously at Allison's house next door. Her friend's car wasn't there, which meant she could slip in without being seen. After everything she'd been through, she did not need Allison's drama right now.

On her way up the front steps she admired the potted plants, and the sign. Inner Beauty Spa—Making the Most of What You've Got, Naturally.

The door knocker was a gargoyle's head with a brass ring in its toothy grin. Maggie's addition, she was sure, and it had Leslie grinning, too. She tapped it several times and as she waited for Maggie to answer the door, she wondered why she hadn't considered buying a house in one of Collingwood Station's older neighborhoods. She had always loved this neighborhood, and she'd spent a lot of time here since Allison and John had moved into the house next door. Maggie's place had a lot of character and so did Brent's. Her town house was boring and uninspired, and it had no personality.

A lot like Gerald, now that she thought about it. And a sad reflection of her.

She had never been to Nick's apartment, but she had a feeling that someday soon he'd be living here. With someone he was madly in love with, and who was madly in love with him. For the first time she could remember, she wanted what Nick had.

The door opened and Maggie's warm, welcoming hug immediately made her feel at home. "I'm so glad you decided to come. An hour from now you'll feel like a million bucks, I guarantee it, and this will give us a chance to get to know each other better."

"Thanks for inviting me. I was so anxious to get home this morning, and then after I spent an hour there by myself, I couldn't wait to get away."

"What were you doing for that hour?"

"Just a little tidying up."

"I'll bet you were packing up Gerald's things, weren't you?"

"How did you know?"

Maggie shrugged. "It's what I would have done."

Except Maggie probably would have thrown his stuff into the yard instead of packing it in a box and stashing it securely in the den.

"I'm so glad you're here," Maggie said. "I had a feeling you'd come so I went ahead and prepared everything we'd need."

Leslie already loved this woman's unabashed self-confidence and nonjudgmental attitude.

"Have a look around while I get set up." Maggie disappeared down the hallway, apparently to the kitchen.

Leslie stepped into the spa and immediately fell in love with the place. Stained glass windows filtered the sunlight and added warmth to the beige and purple walls. Many of the original details had been retained, including the ornate crystal chandelier and the wide mantel over the fireplace, decorated with flowers, candles and a pewter urn. The concept was clearly Maggie's, but there was the same high-quality workmanship that had impressed her about Brent's place. The three of them—Brent, Nick and Maggie—must have had a lot of fun creating this space.

Maggie returned with a tray filled with an assortment of white ceramic bowls and spray bottles, and set it on a modern-looking stainless steel cart. "Come and take a seat over here."

Leslie sat in the salon chair and Maggie swung her to face the mirror, then draped a purple cape over her.

"Your skin is flawless so I'm going to start with an oatmeal scrub," she said, adjusting the height and angle of the chair. "It's a very mild exfoliant."

Leslie lay back in the chair and closed her eyes as Maggie gently massaged the mixture into her skin. She could practically feel the stress oozing out of every pore in her body.

"I think it's wonderful that you were staying with Brent," Maggie said. "Allison said he's had a thing for you since you were kids."

Leslie opened her eyes and stared up at Maggie, trying to think of a response. She needn't have bothered, though, because Maggie wasn't finished.

"Can I be honest?" she asked.

Leslie couldn't imagine her being anything else, so she nodded.

"When I met you and Gerald a couple of weeks ago, I knew you weren't right for each other."

Leslie's throat went tight. "What makes you say that?" she finally managed to ask.

"I'm sure you've heard that old saying, that opposites attract. Well, it's true. Look at me and Nick. He's very grounded and I'm…" She laughed. "Well, not so grounded."

Leslie closed her eyes again and decided there was no point in trying to take part in Maggie's one-sided conversation. She was thrilled that Maggie and Nick were so happy, but she didn't see what that had to do with her.

"Okay, now I'll wash off the scrub with warm water and

use an almond cleanser. This will unclog your pores and leave your skin feeling totally soft and smooth."

"It smells wonderful."

"That's the bonus of using natural products. Their fragrances add a holistic aromatherapy component to a spa treatment."

"I see."

"Now where were we?" Maggie asked. "Oh, right. Opposites. Look at Allison and John. He's very practical and down-to-earth and Allison is all about appearances."

Leslie smiled at that.

"I meant that in a good way. She's completely devoted to her family and her home, and she'll do everything in her power to make them the best they can be."

Leslie had known Allison all her life and had never thought of her that way, but Maggie was absolutely right. Allison was also a devoted friend, and it had been selfish of Leslie not to call and let her know what had happened, and that she was all right.

Maggie carefully rinsed the cleanser off Leslie's face and patted it dry. "Doesn't that feel wonderful?" she asked.

"Heavenly. You were so right, I needed this."

"But the best is yet to come." She picked up a small bowl and stirred its contents. "This is a chocolate facial mask."

"Chocolate?"

"It sounds ridiculously decadent, but you're going to love it. It does a fantastic job of moisturizing the skin."

Leslie loved the feel and smell of the mixture. "It smells good enough to eat."

"That's what Nick says about some of the beauty products I make."

Leslie opened her eyes in time to catch the sparkle in Maggie's.

"Lucky for him, and me, some of them are."

Bordering on too much information, Leslie thought.

Maggie seemed to think so, too. "I'm sorry. I have a habit of saying too much sometimes. That needs to stay on for ten minutes, so while we wait I can give you a hand treatment. But first, close your eyes and I'll cover them with these cool compresses."

"What are those?" Leslie asked as she inhaled.

"Peppermint tea bags."

Chocolate *and* peppermint. "I smell like dessert."

Maggie laughed. "If Brent were here, I bet he'd say you look like dessert, too."

Fortunately the heat that spread across her face was covered by the mask. Maggie was right, though. It sounded exactly like something he might say. She could even imagine the look in his eyes as he said it.

She heard the sound of a chair on wheels being moved beside her, and Maggie sitting on it.

"Did you spend a lot of time with Nick and Brent when they were working here?" Leslie asked, hoping to keep the subject away from her and Brent, for a while at least. And far away from the topic of opposites. She already knew that she and Brent were, and she didn't particularly want to find out why Maggie thought she and Gerald weren't.

"I did. I made lunch for them every day, and of course they checked with me as they did things because I had such a clear vision for what I wanted."

"It was a good vision. The place is beautiful."

"Thank you. We had a lot of fun and I'm going to miss them. Well, I have a feeling I'll be seeing a lot of Nick, but I'll miss Brent. He was always joking around or pulling some kind of prank."

"Really?" *That's what was different about him,* Leslie realized. He'd always teased and played practical jokes, but for the past few days he'd seemed much more serious. She'd attributed it to maturity but according to Maggie, that wasn't the case. Now it seemed as though he'd been treating her with kid gloves.

"Did he tell you what he did to my gardening shoes?" Maggie asked.

Leslie shook her head.

"I was carrying the lunch tray outside and stopped to slip my feet into them. When I tried to take a step, I nearly fell over, sandwiches and all." She was laughing again. "He had nailed them to the floor of the porch!"

And that was classic Brent Borden, Leslie thought. It was always about getting a laugh and never about the consequences.

"I thought we'd die laughing. Nick didn't think it was funny, but I did. I can't imagine going through life without a sense of humor, so I'm helping Nick work on his."

Good luck. The Durrance family was known for many things, but a sense of humor was not one of them.

"Hand massages are so relaxing, don't you think?" Maggie asked.

Leslie was so relaxed, she felt as though she were floating. "They are. Thank you for suggesting it."

"My pleasure. So what are your plans for the rest of the week?"

"I have to return the wedding gifts, and I'd like to get that out of the way as quickly as possible. I also have to help a friend find a place to live. She used to be our housekeeper, but she's retired now."

"What sort of place is she looking for?" Maggie asked.

Leslie didn't know, exactly, other than it had to be affordable. "I'm not sure. The old building she was living in on Railway Avenue is being torn down and she has no place to go. Right now—" She hesitated, not sure how much to say to Maggie, until she reminded herself this woman was not going to pass judgment. "Right now she's at the homeless shelter. I was there yesterday with Brent—he had to repair the laundry equipment. I couldn't have imagined running into anyone I know, but there she was."

"How awful," Maggie said. She slathered something warm and pasty on Leslie's hand, covered it with a plastic bag and moved the chair around to her other side. "I'd offer to have her here, but the bedrooms upstairs are still crammed with all the furniture that used to be down here and I haven't had a chance to organize any of it."

"Oh. Thank you for offering but…ah…I was planning to have her stay with me while we look for an apartment for her." Which couldn't have been further from the truth. Leslie was mortified that the idea hadn't crossed her mind until Maggie, a complete stranger, had offered Hannah a temporary place to stay. Why hadn't she thought of it herself? She had a huge town house, complete with a guest room on the main floor. Hannah wouldn't even have to manage the stairs if she wasn't up to them.

"Good for you," Maggie said, as though she hadn't been the one to think of it first. "And it'll probably be nice to have some company right now. It'll help keep your mind off things."

If Leslie hadn't been lying there slathered in chocolate and peppermint and with her hands wrapped in plastic, she would have hugged Maggie. This was exactly what she needed, and exactly what Hannah needed.

A win-win situation, she thought, then inwardly cringed at the sound of it. That was something Gerald would have said.

What would Brent call it? He'd probably say it was a helluva good idea. And that it was.

"Okay," Maggie said, lifting the tea bags off Leslie's eyes. "I'll wash off the mask and the hand treatment, apply some moisturizer and then you're good to go."

Leslie blinked a few times as her eyes adjusted to the light. "Thank you very much. This has been wonderful."

"Anytime. You'll be one of my preferred clients," Maggie said, removing the cape.

Leslie liked the sound of that. There was something about Maggie she liked a lot, and she couldn't remember the last time a conversation had been so enlightening, and on so many levels.

She stood and Maggie walked with her to the front door.

"How much do I owe you?" Leslie asked.

"I wouldn't dream of accepting anything. I invited you, and this is for you, too."

Leslie accepted a small, handmade sachet.

"Those are lavender bath salts, so you can have a nice, relaxing soak in the tub when you get home."

"Thank you. This is very generous of you, but next time I come, I insist on paying."

"And I'll let you," Maggie said, smiling broadly. "And meanwhile you might tell some of your friends about me."

"Of course I will." If she still had any.

She said goodbye to Maggie and let herself out, pausing for a moment at the gate. Maggie had been right. She did feel like a million dollars. In fact, she felt like a different person. She glanced next door and saw Allison's car parked in the driveway. It was time to stop thinking about herself, and hope her friend would understand why she hadn't called.

LESLIE HAD BEEN anxious to get to the shelter so her visit with Allison had been brief, but long enough to know that all her worrying over Allison's phone messages had been unfounded. Her friend had been genuinely concerned about her, and her real anger had been intended for Gerald. All was well, and they agreed to meet for coffee later in the week.

At the homeless shelter, Leslie pulled her BMW into the spot where Brent had parked yesterday. The same group of men—at least, they looked like the same group—was sitting on the steps, exactly where they'd been yesterday. Today she found them less intimidating.

"Good afternoon, gentlemen."

"Afternoon," one of them replied. Another tipped his hat.

She wove her way between them and up to the front door. She had hoped to get in and out without encountering Colleen Borden, but she wasn't that lucky. After she was buzzed in, Brent's mother was the first person she bumped into.

Colleen was clearly surprised to see her. "Leslie? What are you doing here?"

"Oh, hello. Nice to see you again." For once she felt as though she had the upper hand and she tried to keep her voice sounding breezy but professional. "Is Hannah still here?"

That question earned her a somewhat scornful look. "I wish I could say we'd solved the homeless crisis overnight but yes, she's still with us."

Leslie refused to be baited. "Well, Hannah's crisis has been. I'm taking her home with me."

"I don't suppose you'd like to take a few more while you're at it."

The woman was a laugh a minute. She'd dropped her sarcastic tone from yesterday, though, and she seemed uncharacteristically defeated. "I'm afraid Hannah is all I can manage right now. Is something wrong?"

"You could say that. We received this in the mail today." She handed a sheet of paper to her.

Leslie unfolded it and scanned the contents. It was an eviction notice. The building was slated for demolition and the Helping Hands Foundation that ran the shelter had until the end of the year to vacate the premises.

"I'm so sorry," she said. From what Brent had told her about his mother, she knew the woman was completely devoted to this cause. "Maybe you'll find a new location that doesn't need so many repairs."

Colleen took the letter from her. "This place is being torn down to build condos or a mall or something, just like every other old building in this town. There are no new locations. By Christmastime, these people won't just be homeless, they won't have a shelter to go to, either."

"Is the situation really that hopeless?"

"I'm afraid so. We can barely come up with enough money to pay the rent on this place. Even if we are lucky enough to find another building, and that's a big if, the rent will be a lot higher."

"You could hold a fund-raising event," Leslie suggested. "That would help."

Colleen gave an exaggerated sigh. "We've tried that and I'm afraid it wasn't very successful."

"What if I offered to organize it?"

For once Colleen was speechless.

"I need to go look for Hannah, but I'll tell you what. I'll jot down a few ideas about a fund-raiser and come back tomorrow to discuss it with you. By then I'll have had a chance to launder the clothes I borrowed. I'll bring those with me, too."

"Oh. Okay."

"Will ten o'clock work for you?"

"Ten. Sure."

"Great. I'll see you then." She couldn't help feeling a little smug at finally doing something that seemed to impress Brent's mother. Or at least catch her off guard enough to soften her hostility.

She walked into the lounge and, sure enough, Hannah was there. She seemed even more surprised to see her than Colleen had been. "Leslie! I knew you'd come back to see me, but I didn't expect it to be so soon."

Leslie sat on the old sofa and took the woman's workworn hands in hers. "I came to take you home. That is, I hope you'll come with me."

"You always were a sweet girl and I appreciate your thinking about me, but this isn't necessary. I'll be fine."

"I hope you'll reconsider. I have plenty of room. You'll have your own bedroom with a private bath. It's on the main floor, so you don't have to worry about stairs."

Hannah looked indignant. "Until last month, my apartment was on the third floor of a building and there was no elevator. I can manage stairs if I have to."

Leslie smiled at the way Hannah had risen to the challenge. "Then you'll come with me?"

Still the woman hesitated.

"You'd actually be doing me a real favor," Leslie said. "To be honest, my place seems too big for just me and…" She paused before using her trump card.

"And you don't want to be alone right now," Hannah said, after listening to the details of the wedding that wasn't.

Leslie nodded.

"If I say yes, we need to be clear about who's doing who the favor here."

"Whatever you say."

"And I'll earn my keep. I'm no freeloader, you know."

She knew Hannah would never agree to being her guest. "You can work away to your heart's content."

"And help with the cooking."

"I'm a very good cook, you know." She leaned forward and gently squeezed Hannah's hands. "I learned from the best. And I have a cleaning woman who comes in once a week, so there isn't a lot to do."

Hannah's eyes narrowed. "I've never been waited on in my life. You'll have to tell that cleaning woman to stay out of my room."

Leslie pressed her lips together to keep from smiling. "Your room is off-limits. And you and I can cook together. It'll be fun."

"It sounds wonderful," Hannah said, finally conceding. "This place isn't a whole lot of fun."

"Then let's go tell Colleen you're coming with me."

"She's been helping me look for a place of my own, but we haven't found anything I can afford."

"I'll help, too. Meanwhile, you can stay with me as long as you need to." She could stay forever, but Leslie knew she'd never agree to that.

"You'll change your mind about having an old lady in the house when all those young friends of yours start coming around."

Leslie was sure that even Hannah would find her parties tame. "Let's get your things. My car isn't very big, but we can take what we can and I'll send for the rest."

"I don't have much. I gave some things to a friend and left the rest behind."

"Oh, Hannah. That's terrible. Do you think we'll still be able to get them back?"

"They're just things. I have my health and all my faculties. And my good friends," she said, patting Leslie's hand. "No one can take those away from me."

Leslie leaned over and gave her a hug. "You're so right, Hannah. Thank you for reminding me."

Spending those two days with Brent, seeing the work Colleen did here at the shelter and meeting Hannah again were exactly what she'd needed to regain some perspective. She stood and helped Hannah to her feet.

"Let's go home." Tomorrow she could worry about winning over Colleen Borden.

FOR MOST of the morning Brent kept himself busy by washing the breakfast dishes, taking Max for a walk and mowing the lawn. At lunchtime he poured himself a cup of leftover coffee and stuck it in the microwave. While he waited for it to heat up, Max wandered in and sat on his haunches, staring up at him.

"What are you looking at?"

Max whined softly.

"Tell me about it," he said, giving the dog a scruff on the head. "I miss her, too."

Max's gaze didn't waver.

"It's not my fault she left."

But it was. He'd moved too fast last night, and this morning she'd decided it was safer to take her chances with Collingwood Station's tongue-waggers than to stay with him. Now he didn't know what to do with himself, and neither did Max.

Too bad Nick had decided to put off starting the new job till tomorrow. If Brent had been thinking more clearly, he'd have offered to go in on his own and get things started. But he didn't have the plans or the keys, and no way was he calling Nick to get them. So he was stuck at home in a house that suddenly felt too big and too empty.

The microwave pinged. He took out the coffee and carried it into the room Leslie had slept in and looked around. She had offered to strip the bed and wash the sheets but he'd told her to leave it. The bed had been made and his clothes were neatly folded and piled on the end. He picked up the shirt, wanting to bury his face in it, but resisted the urge. He'd already tortured himself enough.

Damn it. He shouldn't have rushed her. If he hadn't, she'd still be here. Now the most he could hope for was that he hadn't completely blown his chances and that she'd agree to see him again.

He dropped the shirt back on the bed and opened the top drawer of the dresser. If she had left something behind, he'd have a good reason to call her and return it.

But the drawer was empty. So were the others. He opened the closet.

Aha.

Her wedding dress.

Did he dare to hope that she had left it here on purpose? A reason to come back and pick it up? Yeah, right. In his dreams.

He could call and offer to drop off the dress at her place, but what if she didn't want it? He'd have to come up with another excuse to see her.

Better not to risk a phone call. He'd wait a couple of days, or at least till tomorrow—wouldn't want to look too eager— and then he'd take it to her place in person.

He let the silk slip through his fingers. In spite of being soaking wet when he'd found her, she had looked stunning in this dress. Too beautiful to be marrying a jerk like Gerald Bedford.

Problem was, she didn't have the greatest opinion of Brent Borden right now, either. It would definitely be better to give her some space and a little time, and a chance to put last night behind them.

Next time they made out—and he hoped there'd *be* a next time—he'd let her call the shots.

He went into his bedroom and picked up the shoes she'd left there yesterday when she'd gone in to console Max. Hands down, they were the sexiest shoes he'd ever seen. She had been carrying them when he'd picked her up so he hadn't had the pleasure of seeing her in them. He couldn't imagine how women walked in heels this high, but he was damned glad they'd figured it out.

Max had sure done a number on them. They weren't the first pair of shoes he'd chewed but judging by the name of the Italian designer on the insole, they were the most expensive.

Brent sighed. He was making a mental note of the size and wondering if she'd bought them in the city or if Collingwood Station had a store that sold this kind of shoes when his cell phone rang. Before he answered, he put the shoes back in the closet and firmly closed the door so Max couldn't get at them again.

The call was from his mother at the shelter. Another disaster, no doubt.

"Hey, Mom. What's happening?"

"Are you at work?"

"No, I'm at home. Something came up and Nick decided we'd start the new job tomorrow."

"I see. Well, you'll never guess who just dropped by the shelter."

He was not in the mood for guessing games. "You're right," he said. "Why don't you save us both some time and tell me?"

"Oh, my. Somebody got up on the wrong side of the bed this morning."

"Mom, don't start with me."

He recognized the laughter in her voice, even though he couldn't hear it. "Leslie Durrance," she said.

"What about her?"

"She was just here."

Good thing his mother hadn't made him guess because Leslie would have been one of the last people he would have named.

"Is that right?" he asked casually. "I'm sure she wanted to see Hannah and return the clothes she borrowed."

"She said she'd wash them and bring them back tomorrow, and she didn't just want to visit with Hannah."

Brent sighed. His mother was enjoying this way too much. "Fine. I give up. Why was she there?"

"She took Hannah with her. Packed the woman's things into the trunk of her Beemer and away they went."

He had to hand it to Leslie. When she made up her mind to do something, she didn't waste any time. "Good for her. If you ever bothered to listen to me, you would have known she's not some spoiled rich kid." To use his mother's own words.

"I'll reserve my judgment on that. Although something else interesting happened while she was here."

"What was that?"

"It's bad news, but Leslie offered to help." That statement was followed by more silence.

"And the bad news would be…"

"A developer has purchased all the buildings on the block. The foundation received an eviction notice this morning. We have to be out of here in a few months."

"How much time does that give you?"

"Till Christmas."

"That's not good." He knew how much affordable real estate was available to an organization like Helping Hands. None. He also knew that his mother would go to extremes to save the shelter. "What are you going to do?" he asked cautiously, hoping she wouldn't tell him that she was taking out a second mortgage on her house. It wouldn't be the first time she'd suggested it, but he'd always managed to talk her out of it. This time, given the severity of the situation, he might not be able to.

"Believe it or not, Leslie offered to do some fund-raising. Says she has lots of contacts and that she'll be able to raise a significant amount of money."

"You just said you didn't like her."

"No, I didn't. I said I'd reserve judgment."

How was that not the same thing? "If that's how you feel, then maybe you shouldn't take advantage of her." Although Leslie's help might save his mother from financial ruin.

"I'm not. She volunteered."

He sighed. He could hear the determination in his mother's voice, so he hated to burst her bubble—or Leslie's for that matter—but it was going to take a lot more than a bake sale and a raffle to cover what would certainly be a hefty rent increase for another facility. "Well, good for her, and you. I hope this works out."

"So do I. She took Hannah to her place and is getting her settled in today. Tomorrow she and I are meeting to discuss the possibilities."

"What time?" he asked.

"Don't even think about it."

"What?"

"Showing up here just so you can see her."

"I'm working tomorrow. Why would I go to the shelter?"

"You were working on Saturday but you still ended up at the church."

Brent sighed. There was no winning when it came to these kinds of discussions with his mother. He knew better than even to try. "I won't be at the shelter tomorrow. If I want to see Leslie, I'll call her."

"And you think she'll go out with you?"

"We're friends. I'm not going to ask her out." Besides, he'd rather stay in, and delivering her wedding dress and a new pair of shoes would be the perfect way to do that. "I'm sure she'll do a great job of raising money for you, so you might want to try being a little nicer to her."

That suggestion was met with silence, and he readied himself for a lecture. This time, she surprised him. "You know, it's not so much her that I don't like, but it was the way she always treated you."

"Are you kidding me?" He'd thought this animosity stemmed from the two of them serving on the redevelopment committee together. "This is about her not going out with me in high school?"

"It's about her thinking you weren't good enough."

"Mom, it wasn't just me. Leslie didn't date anybody in high school." When would she have found the time? She'd been too busy paving the road to Harvard. But that didn't change the fact that he *wasn't* good enough for her—nobody was—but at least there hadn't been any competition.

"Oh," his mother said. "I didn't know that."

"Now you do, so can you ease up on her? Please?"

"I'm sorry, honey. Maybe I've been overreacting."

Geez, you think? But he let her continue.

"I just don't want to see you get hurt again."

"Mom, I can take care of myself."

"So, how did it go with her this weekend? Is she starting to thaw out a little?"

"Mom! Let it go." As soon as he said it, he could sense her amusement. No matter what he tried to keep from her, his life always seemed to be an open book.

"Whatever you say, dear. Just promise me one thing."

"What's that?"

"Don't rush into anything."

It was a little late for that. "Sure thing. Listen, I'm sure you're busy, and Max is sitting at the door." He was actually sprawled in the sunlight streaming through the French doors, but technically it was true. "I think he needs to go for a walk." That was an out-and-out lie, but he'd never been very good at wrapping up one of these calls from his mother.

"Okay. I'll call you tomorrow after I meet with Leslie." He didn't bother to remind her that he'd be at work tomorrow. It wouldn't stop her, anyway.

THE FIRST MORNING back in her own home and her own bed, Leslie woke to the smell of coffee.

Hannah! Obviously the woman was still an early bird.

Leslie quickly climbed out of bed and slipped into her pink silk robe and a pair of mules. She found Hannah in the kitchen, cleaning up her baking dishes.

"Good morning! You're up early. And already hard at work, I see."

"G'morning to you. It's a joy to be back in such a well-stocked kitchen." Hannah poured a cup of coffee and slid it across the island to her. "And to have someone to cook for."

Leslie slid onto a stool and wrapped her hands around the cup. "Thank you."

The phone rang, and they both glanced at the clock. "I'll take that in the den," Leslie said.

She checked the caller ID. It was her mother. "Sorry, Mother. It's too early for this." She waited a minute after the phone stopped ringing, then went back to the kitchen.

"I hope nothing's wrong," Hannah said.

"Everything's fine. It was just someone calling to see if I'm all right. Now you have to tell me what's in the oven," she said, hoping her guess was correct.

"One of your favorites, if I remember."

"They smell heavenly. No one in the world makes cinnamon buns as good as yours."

Hannah laughed. "Here's hoping I haven't lost my touch."

"That would be impossible. But you're here as my guest, not my housekeeper. I want you to relax and take things easy."

Hannah placed her hands on her hips. "It's a hard-hearted girl who'd deny a poor old woman like me the pleasure of working in such a kitchen."

Leslie laughed. "Hard-hearted? I hate to think what Colleen Borden would say if she showed up here and found you slaving over a hot stove."

"I think she'd be happy that I have a roof over my head and a big, comfortable guest room to sleep in."

Unless Colleen found someplace to relocate the shelter to by Christmastime, there would be a lot of people who weren't so fortunate. But there was no sense in worrying Hannah about that. "Considering what you've been through in the past month, I'm thrilled to see you in such good health. We want to keep it that way."

"And I like to keep busy. So you can do whatever it is you

need to do, and I'll cook. Nothing would make me happier." Hannah opened the oven door and peeked inside, then reached for a pair of pot holders. "They're done."

Leslie smiled. She considered herself to be a good cook, but she'd never acquired Hannah's ability to simply know when something was "done." She took a rack out of a cupboard near the stove and set it on the counter. Hannah slid the buns onto it, and within minutes they were sitting in the breakfast nook together.

"I'm so glad we met again," Leslie said. "It was a lucky thing that I went to the shelter with Brent the other day."

"I say it was providence. Not that I minded being there," Hannah was quick to add. "I'm grateful they took me in. The shelter's a lot better than the street. It'll be a sad day for Collingwood Station when that place has to close."

"You heard about that?"

"Bad news always travels fast."

Wasn't that the truth? "Yesterday Colleen told me they have to be out of the building by Christmas, and she has no idea where they're going to go."

"A lot of people rely on that place. I didn't know how many until I had to go there myself."

"I told her I'll do what I can to help. There are a few people I can call about finding a new building, but it sounds as though the foundation is hard up for money. I've been mulling over ideas for raising funds."

"When it comes to that sort of thing, I'll bet you're the best there is."

"Thanks. I wasn't sure how Colleen would respond when I offered to help, given that she's not all that crazy about me, but she seemed enthusiastic. I'm going over there today to discuss my ideas with her."

"Now that you have a common goal, I'm sure the two of you will get along like a house on fire."

"I hope you're right." As for getting along with Brent's mother, Leslie decided a wait-and-see approach would be wisest. She was debating whether or not to indulge in another cinnamon bun when the doorbell rang.

Damn it. Who would come here at—she glanced at the clock—7:57? The most likely candidates were Gerald and her mother, and she wasn't ready to see either of them. Would Gerald be likely to show up? No. Which narrowed the possibilities to one.

"Would you like me to get that?" Hannah asked.

"No!" She stood and put a hand on Hannah's shoulder. "Thanks, but no. You're my guest, remember? Sit and enjoy your coffee. I'll be right back."

She peered through the peephole in the front door and sighed. Her mother stood on the other side, every silver hair in place, looking like a sergeant major in a smog-colored business suit. Lydia Durrance was the last person in the world Leslie wanted to see right now. Make that the second-last person. If it had been Gerald standing out there, she wouldn't dare open the door. Since it was her mother, she didn't dare not to.

The bell rang again.

She released the dead bolt, pasted on as cheerful a smile as she could manage and swung the door open.

"Good morning, Mother. What brings you by?"

Lydia Durrance huffed her disapproval and brushed past her into the foyer, making Leslie instantly regret not stopping at good morning. "Don't be glib, Leslie. It's most unbecoming, especially under the circumstances."

Leslie sighed. "I am little surprised to see you this early."

"I came as soon as I heard you'd come out of hiding. And since you won't return your calls, or even answer them, I had no choice but to come here. We need to talk."

Leslie wondered, in passing, who had ratted her out. Not Nick, that's for sure. But given that her mother had likely had her spies out searching for her, she should consider herself lucky her mother hadn't shown up yesterday. "Would you like to come in for coffee? I should tell you that I have company. We were just finishing breakfast."

Her mother's narrow-eyed scrutiny made her uncomfortable. "Is it Gerald?"

"God, no! How could you even think that? Surely you must have heard—"

"I'm not interested in discussing what you think he might have done."

"Mother, I don't 'think' anything." She lowered her voice so Hannah wouldn't hear. "I saw him with Candice, right there in the church."

"And it didn't occur to you to try to work things out?"

"Work out what? Which nights he'd be home and which he'd spend with her?"

"Don't be ridiculous. He was probably just sowing the last of his wild oats."

Leslie could not believe what she was hearing. "Then he should have sown them before he asked me to marry him. And not with one of my *former* best friends."

That seemed to thaw her mother's icy demeanor. "I agree with you on that point. He should have known better than that."

Surely she wasn't suggesting that it would be okay for a husband to have an affair with a stranger? Was she implying that Leslie's father had…

No! She had admired and respected her father more than anyone she had ever known, and at that moment she almost hated her mother for making her question his integrity.

"If you'd like to come in for coffee, I'll be happy to discuss whatever you came to discuss…except Gerald. I have nothing to say to him or about him."

"Who's this guest of yours, then?"

"Hannah."

Her mother's shrug indicated the name meant nothing to her.

"Hannah Greene? She was your housekeeper for, oh, I don't know, several decades. Surely you remember her."

"Of course I do. Finding a replacement after she retired was not an easy task. She isn't working for you, is she?"

"Of course not. I don't need a housekeeper." Leslie hesitated, not wanting to give her mother any of the details about her two-day hideaway with Brent. Since she hadn't mentioned it, Leslie felt it was safe to assume that her mother had no idea where she'd been, and she intended to keep it that way. "I discovered that her apartment building is being demolished and she had no place to go, so I invited her to stay with me for a few days. Actually, she's welcome to stay as long as necessary."

"How kind of you. I'm sure she appreciates your charity, but I don't care to discuss family business in front of anyone."

"At least come in and say hello. You can have coffee and one of Hannah's cinnamon buns. Remember those? They're fresh out of the oven."

But by the time they made their way to the kitchen, Hannah had disappeared. Leslie peeked down the hallway and saw that the door to the guest room was closed. She indulged in a sly smile. Her mother might not have wanted to see Hannah, but it looked as though the feeling was mutual.

While her mother settled herself into the breakfast nook, Leslie poured her a cup of coffee and set a clean plate and a napkin on the place mat in front of her. "You really should try one of the cinnamon buns. They're delicious."

"Of course." She peeked under the cloth cover that was keeping them warm. "I've never been able to find anyone who could make them the way Hannah did."

"And still does," Leslie said, gently reminding her mother that the woman wasn't dead.

"So it seems." She delicately wiped her fingers on the

napkin and looked at Leslie. "Now, we have more important things to discuss."

"Such as?"

"How we're going to handle this botched wedding." But there was no missing her unspoken question. You have to ask?

"Everything's been taken care of. I called the country club yesterday to express my regrets. And to settle my account." After she'd talked to Colleen Borden yesterday, she'd been mulling over ideas for the fund-raiser, so she had wanted to know if the country club had any dates open in the next few weeks.

"And the gifts?"

Leslie bit back an angry remark. "I'll return them, of course."

"Good." Her mother took a bite of the pastry and nodded her approval. "These are delicious."

"I'll be sure to tell Hannah."

"I'm sure you will. Now, we need to do some serious damage control, and we need to do it fast."

Damage control? God, this wasn't politics. But Leslie did her best to offer a sweet smile. "What do you have in mind?"

"A social function. A party of some kind. I am not letting the Bedfords have the upper hand. We can have it at the house, since the gardens look particularly good right now. We'll invite everybody, of course."

Her mother's expression told her that she expected to do battle over this, but at that moment Leslie's plan for a fund-raising event for the shelter solidified. She hadn't thought of holding it at her mother's place, but of course it would be perfect. For now all her mother needed to know was that there was going to be a party. By the time Leslie filled her in on the plan, it would be too late for her to back out.

And of course, Gerald was welcome to join the festivities, providing he brought his checkbook.

"It's very generous of you to host a party," Leslie said. "But will you please let me take care of everything else? I think it will be good, you know, to have something to keep myself busy and not dwell on the way this turned out."

"Of course, dear." For once, her mother couldn't seem to think of anything to say.

"More coffee?"

"Thank you, but no. I'm on my way to a meeting of the opera society at ten and I have a few errands to run before that."

They both stood and Leslie accompanied her mother to the front door. Her mother leaned toward her slightly and sent an air kiss in her direction.

She remembered how Brent had hugged his mother and wished she could do the same. It would make both of them uncomfortable, though. For now it seemed that Lydia Durrance believed her daughter was being her usual compliant self. The last thing Leslie wanted to do was raise any suspicion that she might be up to something.

"You'll let me know as soon as you've decided on a date for the party?" her mother asked. "And a guest list?"

"I'll call you in a couple of days. It won't take me long to work out the details." If Leslie had learned anything from her mother, it was how to throw a party at the drop of a hat. Of course, her mother's good works were always on behalf of the privileged, like the Women's League and the Collingwood Station Opera Society.

This party would be different. She could hardly wait to get started, and she could hardly wait to see her mother's reaction when she found out she was hosting a fund-raiser to help the homeless.

Chapter Ten

Brent parked his truck in the alley behind the new job site. The pile of lumber he'd unloaded on Saturday was waiting, and so was Nick. They hadn't had a chance to talk when Nick had picked up Leslie yesterday, and Brent was in no mood for talking today.

Nick was leaning against the front of his truck, ankles crossed and arms folded. "You're late," he said.

Brent pocketed his keys. "Since when do we punch a clock?"

"Somebody got up on the wrong side of the bed."

"So people keep telling me."

Nick grinned at him. "My sister doesn't usually have that effect on people."

"I'm ten minutes late. Your sister left yesterday. What does one have to do with the other?"

"You tell me."

Brent grabbed his toolbox out of the back of the truck. No way was he telling Nick he was late because he'd driven past Leslie's town house. It had been a dumb thing to do, even dumber than driving by the church, but at least this time he hadn't been found out. "It's not a big deal," he said. "I had to run an errand, that's all. So, how are things with you?"

"Good."

"And Maggie?"

"Maggie's good."

"Good."

Nick laughed. "Hey, I didn't mean to give you such a hard time. And I haven't thanked you for rescuing my sister."

Brent wondered exactly how much Leslie had told him. Not everything, he hoped. "I was just glad I could help."

"For sure. Lucky that you happened to be driving by the church on Saturday morning."

"You said you weren't going to give me a hard time."

"Yeah. I lied."

"Okay. I drove by the church. What's wrong with that? It's not like I was stalking her."

Nick was laughing again. "The jury's still out on that."

"Very funny." But now he really hoped no one had seen him this morning. Especially not Leslie.

"So, the two of you must have had an interesting couple of days holed up together."

Brent shook his head. "If anybody else made that kind of insinuation about your sister, you'd punch his lights out."

"I'm not insinuating anything. I know my sister, and that's not her style. And if something had happened, you wouldn't be in such a foul mood."

"Are we going to work today, or just stand around talking about my foul mood?" Which was about to get fouler.

"Sure. We can work and talk at the same time."

Great, Brent thought. Let the good times roll.

LESLIE FOLLOWED a volunteer into a small, dingy back room at the shelter. It wasn't much of an office, but it wasn't unexpected.

The middle-aged woman hovered in the doorway. "Colleen's on the phone but she said she'll be with you as soon as she can. Would you like some coffee while you wait?"

"Oh, thanks, but no thanks." If the coffee was like everything else in this place, it would only be marginally acceptable.

She took a chair at a battered old folding table that served as a makeshift desk. The plywood surface had lost most of its finish and was covered with stains and carved initials. She glanced down at the drab linoleum. She set the bag of clothing on the floor but held her briefcase on her lap. While she waited, she took out a file folder and flipped through her notes.

Colleen hurried in a few minutes later, wheeled an ancient office chair up to the table and sat down. "Sorry to keep you waiting. I was on the phone with a reporter from the newspaper who wants to do a story about the shelter having to shut down."

She made it sound so final, and Leslie had no doubt that she'd painted a doom-and-gloom picture for the reporter. "I'm sure you'll have a new place lined up by the time you have to be out of here."

Colleen clearly didn't believe that, and she made no attempt to hide her bitterness. "We both know that's not likely to happen. The redevelopment committee has done what it set out to do. Tear down all the affordable housing in town and replace it with upscale condos and tourist hangouts."

Leslie didn't know how to respond. Maybe she was over-reacting, but it seemed to her the underlying implication was that she was part of the problem. To some extent that might be true, but she couldn't rewrite history. She did, however, have a chance to show Brent's mother that she could be part of the solution.

"I'm sure we…you…will be able to find another facility, and I'd really like to help. I've started to put together a plan for the fund-raising event. It's fairly ambitious, but I think it should be able raise a lot of money."

"You know, this kind of thing is not as easy as you think. We've held fund-raisers in the past and never managed to raise more than a few thousand dollars."

Amateurs. Leslie opened her briefcase and took out several more files, determined to diminish Colleen's skepticism.

"You have been hard at work."

"I found an ideal venue," Leslie said. "And best of all it's free. Once I had that lined up, everything else seemed to fall into place."

"You're telling me someone in this town is doing something out of the goodness of their hearts? That has to be a first."

Leslie smiled at the idea of there being any goodness in her mother's heart. "There's one stipulation. If I tell you where it's going to be, you have to keep it to yourself until I have all the publicity lined up."

Colleen waved a hand at their stark surroundings. "This place is a lifeline for a lot of people. If there's even a remote possibility of finding another building, I won't do anything to jeopardize it."

"Of course you wouldn't. We're going to use my mother's place." She took a sketch out of a folder and set it on the table. "She has a huge property and we can hold it outdoors."

Colleen's gaze wavered a little. "Your mother is Lydia Durrance, right?"

"Yes, she is."

"And she's offered to host an event to raise money for the homeless?"

"Um, not exactly. That's why we need to keep this quiet for a bit."

Colleen gaped at her. "She doesn't know about this?"

"She suggested I throw a party. She thinks...well, none of that matters. It was her idea to have it at her place."

"But she didn't have the homeless in mind when she made that offer."

"No, she didn't." Leslie couldn't imagine anything being further from her mother's mind.

"What happens when she finds out? If she changes her mind, we're...well, we're screwed."

"I know my mother." She just wasn't sure how much she wanted to tell Brent's mother. "She's worried that calling off the wedding didn't look good, so she will *not* back out of the fund-raiser. But I want to have the tickets printed and the advertising in place before I tell her."

Colleen shook her head and rolled her eyes toward the ceiling. "You people are too much."

You people? Stay calm, Leslie. Don't let her get to you.

Sometimes the direct approach was best, and Leslie decided this was one of those times. "I know you don't like me, and I can tell you don't approve of my…" Social circle? She couldn't say that. "Of my family and friends," she said. "But a lot of people will jump at a chance to attend a function at the Durrance estate. If we charge two-fifty per ticket—"

"And you seriously think we can make money?" Colleen's disbelief was unmistakable.

"You think two hundred and fifty dollars isn't enough?"

Colleen stared at her, and for once she was speechless. Surely she hadn't thought… But clearly she had.

"It's a very reasonable price for what we'll be doing. I'm sure we can sell at least two hundred tickets." Leslie watched as Colleen did the mental calculation.

"That's fifty thousand dollars!"

"That's right." She paused and gave Colleen a chance to process that information. "We'll have some expenses, of course, but I've already lined up a few donations. And I think that if we do something really festive, a lot of people are likely to make even bigger cash donations once they're there."

"What do you mean by 'festive'?" Finally there was some interest in her voice.

She took a deep breath before making the plunge. "I thought we could have a Christmas in July theme."

"Christmas? In July?"

Leslie sighed. "Just hear me out. People are always more

generous around the holidays but by Christmastime—the real one—it'll be too late. The shelter needs money now, so we'll have Christmas now."

"And you think people will pay two hundred and fifty dollars to have Christmas in July?"

"Technically it'll be early August, but yes, I believe they will."

Colleen leaned back in her chair and shook her head. "Don't get me wrong. This is very generous of you, but I don't have time to work on this, and the foundation sure doesn't have the capital to float this kind of venture."

It occurred to Leslie that Colleen could probably put a damper on the real Christmas. "I don't want you to worry about any of this. Just keep doing what you do here and let the foundation use what money it has to keep this place running. I have lots of contacts around town and I'm confident that most of what we need will be donated."

"You think people will just give you stuff?"

"Believe it or not, I can be very persuasive."

"I'm sure you can. Not everyone could convince me to go along with a Christmas in July fund-raising event."

Leslie smiled. "People are going to love it, you'll see. A couple of my friends have already offered to help." She glanced over her list. "One last thing. Does the foundation have an accountant? I'd like to have someone you trust to handle all the money." *And please don't let it be Gerald,* she thought.

"Yes, we were lucky enough to find someone willing to take on a pro bono project."

Then it couldn't be Gerald. "That's great. I'll make sure all the financial records are passed on."

"I appreciate that."

Leslie leaned across the table and covered Colleen's hand with hers. "This *will* work," she said. She genuinely wanted to do this, to make a difference for people like Hannah, and now she was just as determined to change Colleen Borden's opinion of her.

"We've never tried anything this ambitious, and I almost can't believe I'm going along with it now, so I hope you're right. A lot of people rely on this place." Colleen pushed herself away from her desk, the squeaky wheels of her chair indicating that the meeting was over. "I have to get back to work. Will you keep me up to date with what you're doing?"

"Of course," Leslie said, tucking her files back in her brief-case. "I'll drop by every couple of days and fill you in on our plans." She picked up the bag of clothing and passed it across the table. "Here are the things Brent borrowed for me. I added a few other things, too."

The extra things were meant to make up for keeping the pink T-shirt and the blue nightgown. Brent had chosen the shirt specifically for her and even if she never wore it again, it would always have that significance. The nightgown was a different matter. She'd worn it to bed last night because it reminded her of him, fresh out of the shower and wearing nothing but a towel. That night his gaze had touched her in a way his hands never could, and she never wanted to forget that.

"Thanks. We can always use donations."

"When I have more time, I'll see what else I can find."

Colleen walked to the front door with her.

Leslie steeled herself to face the heat and the group of men lounging on the steps.

"Will there be a Santa Claus?" Colleen asked.

Leslie turned around and looked at her, wondering if she'd actually heard the question correctly. "I don't know. I hadn't given it any thought."

"If we're going to have Christmas, we should have Santa."

"Oh. Okay. I'll…add that to the list."

She waited until she was out the door and walking down

the block to her car before she gave in to the grin. Colleen was right. What was Christmas without Santa Claus?

BRENT DROVE downtown after work. There was only one shoe store in Collingwood Station that was likely to have a pair of shoes like the ones Max had chewed. He had never set foot in the place and as soon as he walked through the door, he regretted going there. Especially straight from work.

The two young salesclerks could have been fashion models or pop stars. Judging by their expressions, they didn't get a lot of male shoppers covered in plaster and sawdust. Still, they both seemed to want to wait on him.

"Something we can do to help?" the brunette asked.

"Um, yeah. I hope so." He set the bag on the counter and reluctantly took out Leslie's shoes. "I need another pair of shoes like these."

"Oh dear," the girl murmured as she inspected the damage. The other simply tsk-tsked her disapproval.

"My dog chewed them—"

They both looked up at him, eyes wide and accusatory.

"What a shame," the blonde said.

"These are beautiful shoes, and *very* expensive."

"Yeah, well, he'll chew pretty much anything." He hesitated before daring to ask the question that was uppermost on his mind. "So, when you say expensive…"

Like a crime-scene detective, the brunette picked up one of the shoes and examined it. "I think these were four seventy-five, weren't they?" she asked the other woman.

What? There wasn't enough leather in those shoes to make a pair of bootlaces. How in hell did these people have the nerve to charge four hundred and seventy-five bucks for them? That was crazy, and he didn't have that kind of spare change lying around.

He watched her turn the shoe over. "Size seven." She

shook her head and set it back on the counter. "I'll check in the back, but I'm quite certain we don't have any more in that size."

Since there was no way he wanted to unload that kind of money on a pair of shoes, he hoped they didn't. It would save him the embarrassment of having to change his mind. He watched her disappear through a curtained door and smiled at the blonde who remained.

She smiled back, and he could have sworn she was flirting with him. "I love dogs," she gushed. "What kind do you have?"

"A sheepdog."

That seemed to surprise her. "Do you have sheep, too?" she asked, eyeing his work clothes.

He gave her a long look. She was seriously waiting for an answer.

"No," he said. "Just the dog."

"I see." Which meant she was wondering what was responsible for his disheveled appearance if it wasn't sheep.

"I renovate old houses."

"Ahhh."

Luckily the other woman reappeared, shaking her head. "Sorry. We only have a size five and a nine and a half."

"Thanks," he said, hoping his relief wasn't too obvious. He stuffed the shoes back in the bag and headed for the door.

"Your girlfriend has excellent taste. Why don't you bring her in and we'll help her find something else?" the dog lover asked.

Right. Shoe-shopping with Leslie. Somehow he didn't see that happening, especially not at these prices.

He left the store and stood on the sidewalk, debating what to do. Not being able to replace the shoes would weigh on his conscience, but at least he could return the wedding dress in one piece. He'd go home, have a quick shower and head over to Leslie's before he lost his nerve.

As he walked to his truck, a window display in the jewelry

store next door caught his eye. Nothing as fancy as the diamonds that had ended up in his plumbing, but still some beautiful pieces. And no doubt they had some staggering price tags to go with them. As he turned away, though, one ring grabbed his attention. It was set with a single pink stone, simple and elegant. He certainly wasn't in the market for a ring, but somehow that didn't stop him from going inside for a closer look.

LESLIE'S TOWN HOUSE was in one of the new complexes, but the neighborhood was a mix of old and new, much like most of the town. Nick's company had done some restoration work nearby, turning an old warehouse into trendy lofts.

What would she think of him dropping by like this? What if she didn't want the dress back? Like, *really* didn't want it? Maybe she'd tell him to get lost, and take the dress with him.

He rang the doorbell before he lost his nerve.

"Brent, hi. This is a surprise. A good one, though."

She looked completely different from the woman who'd spent two days at his place. Her short dark hair was sleek and styled, and she was wearing makeup. Not so much that it was really obvious, but enough to emphasize the soft brown of her eyes and the curve of her cheekbones. She looked more beautiful than ever.

He held out the dress, realizing too late that he should have put it in something. "You left this at my place."

"Thanks." She took it from him and draped it over her arm. "I remembered it after I got home. I meant to call and make arrangements to get it out of your way, but I've been busy."

"So I hear. That's why I thought I'd drop it off."

"Thanks, but I was in no rush to get it back."

Meaning she saw through his ruse to pay her a visit.

"Hannah and I are making dinner. Would you like to join us?"

He couldn't think of anything he'd like better. Well, maybe one or two things, but those weren't going to happen. "Dinner would be great."

"Then come on in." She opened the closet door and put the dress on a hanger.

He'd found something in the jewelry store that he hoped would make up for not replacing the shoes, but he felt awkward about giving it to her. Better to leave it in his pocket and hope that an opportunity presented itself later. He shrugged out of his jacket and she hung that up, too, then he followed her into the kitchen.

He wasn't a big fan of this type of new construction, but she'd done an impressive job of decorating the place. The muted colors and understated furniture were as elegant as she was.

Hannah was in the kitchen, slicing mushrooms.

"We have a guest for dinner," Leslie said.

The woman looked up and beamed at him. "So I see. How are you, young man?"

"I'm fine, thank you, ma'am. And you?"

"Since this sweet girl insisted I come to stay with her, I can honestly say I've never been better."

Leslie crossed the room and hugged her. "And it's been just like old times, hasn't it?"

"Better than old times."

Brent watched the exchange and was once again struck by what an amazing person Leslie was. He suspected she'd always been like this, which made him wonder why she was so reluctant to let people see this side of her.

"Whatever you're making, it smells great."

"It's boeuf bourguignon. Hannah's is the best there is."

"Sounds as good as it smells." He'd offer to help, but he had no idea what boeuf bourguignon was. Hell, he couldn't even pronounce it.

"What can I do to help?" Leslie asked.

"Nothing," Hannah said, sternly shaking a long-handled spoon at her. "You said you needed to talk to Brent about helping out with this big event of yours. The two of you can sit over there and talk, and I'll eavesdrop while I work. How does that sound?"

"Sounds good to me," he said. "As long as you're sure there's nothing we can do."

Leslie pointed to the glass-topped table in the breakfast nook. "Have a seat. I'll just run upstairs and get my notes." She headed for the stairs, then quickly reappeared. "Would you like something to drink? We made iced tea this afternoon."

"I'll look after that," Hannah said, shooing her out of the room. "She keeps treating me like a visitor and I keep telling her that if I'm going to stay here, I'll earn my keep. And as soon as I find a place of my own, I won't have to bother her anymore."

Brent got the sense she was talking to herself rather than him. She dumped ice into two tall glasses and filled them from a pitcher of tea in the fridge. "Sugar?" she asked.

"No, thanks." He set the glasses on the table and sat down, watching the woman as she went back to work at the granite-topped counter, this time chopping parsley.

She glanced up and caught him watching her. "I hear you have a knack for being in the right place at the right time."

The remark would have caught him off guard if he hadn't seen the twinkle in her bright blue eyes. "It's nice when you get something right, isn't it?"

If only he'd been the right man, everything would have been perfect.

Hannah sent him a sly smile. "Take it slow. She'll come around."

It took a few seconds for her words to register. Was she telling him...

No.

But it sure sounded like it.

Her attention was once again on food preparation, and he wondered if maybe he'd imagined hearing something she hadn't actually said.

He knew what he'd heard, though. Hannah had been given some kind of inside information, which meant that Leslie must have talked to her about him.

Take it slow. Interesting advice. That would be a first for him, but after their disastrous make-out session the other night, he'd been worried he wouldn't have another shot. Taking it slow was infinitely better than having no chance at all. Before he'd figured out how to wheedle a little more information out of Hannah, Leslie came back into the kitchen and set a stack of file folders on the table.

At his place she had seemed not quite unsure of herself, but definitely a little tentative. Not here. Back on her own turf, she was confident and completely in control. Which meant he really needed to watch his step.

Take it slow. She'll come around. He glanced over at Hannah, who was watching him watch Leslie. He smiled at her, and she smiled back.

All right. He needed an ally, and it looked as though he finally had one. He wasn't sure how that might work to his advantage, but it was worth cultivating.

However, he still didn't know how he and Leslie would ever resolve their financial differences. He could have paid for the shoes this afternoon, but he couldn't afford those kinds of things on a regular basis. He was happy with what he had, but he had no right to expect her to lower her standards to match his. She wasn't ostentatious, but she deserved the best. That was one thing Bedford had been able to do for her, and it bugged the hell out of Brent.

"I met with your mother this morning. Have you talked to her?"

"I have." Several times. "Sounds like Christmas in Collingwood Station has come a little early this year."

"So she told you about the theme for the gala? I didn't think she was too crazy about the idea, so I wondered if she'd mention it."

"Oh, I heard all about it. And about the new laundry equipment that was delivered to the shelter today. That was very generous of you." And further underscored the differences in their financial situations.

Her eyebrows knit together slightly. "That's a donation from CS Appliance Center. I arranged for it, but I didn't pay for it. The other day you said the shelter needed new washers and dryers, so I called them and they said no problem."

"My mother didn't mention that. I think she thinks it's from you." No doubt the Appliance Center's generous response had a lot to do with the person who was doing the asking, but if it meant an easier go of it for the shelter, his mother would be all for it.

"There should have been a letter with it. I'll check with her the next time I see her. We'll need to keep a list of donors so we can send thank-you notes after the event."

"I'm sure she found the letter once she recovered from the shock." Judging by the sound of Colleen's voice on the phone early in the afternoon, that was going to take a while. "She's used to getting used clothes and day-old bread, but new appliances don't turn up every day."

"Well, I'm glad I could help make it happen today." She opened a file folder and pulled out a map. "We're holding the event at my mother's place." She showed him the plan of the grounds. "It'll be perfect, don't you think?"

He agreed that it would.

"I've been on the phone all afternoon to businesses around town. Along with the washer and dryer, I think I've managed to line up most of the things we need."

She took a sheet of paper out of a file folder and laid it on the table so he could read it. "The catering company will provide the food at no cost. We'll have to pay the serving staff, but that won't be a huge expense. There'll be a cash bar, so that will take care of itself. Pretty well everything else is on loan from various companies around town. A sound system, lighting, a couple of those big tents in case it rains. What do you think?"

That she might be the most amazing person he'd ever met. "I think you should run for president."

She had an endearing way of scrunching her nose when she wasn't sure what he was talking about, and she was doing it now. "President of what?" she asked.

"The United States."

"Running a country is a lot different from throwing a party."

"Somebody ought to tell that to the politicians," Hannah said.

They all laughed at that.

Leslie poured some more iced tea into her glass and took a sip. "And you already know the best part."

He did? "What's that?"

"The Christmas in July theme."

Right. That hadn't sounded like the best idea to him, but he wasn't going to tell her that. Not while he was reminded of a younger Leslie who had been on every school committee that involved decorating the gym or putting up posters in the hallways.

"You don't think it sounds crazy, do you?" she asked.

From over Leslie's shoulder, he caught a warning glance from Hannah.

"No. Not crazy at all." But he had to struggle to find something appropriate to say. "Christmas without snow will be kind of nice for a change."

Her eyes lit up. "Oh, there will be snow. It'll be the best part, and that's where I need your help."

"Really?" He would agree to practically anything if it meant spending more time with Leslie, but snow in the summertime? He didn't know how he could pull that off.

"I have a lead on one of those snow-making machines they use on film sets. I haven't finalized it yet, but it looks like it'll be a sure thing. I was hoping you and maybe Nick would oversee the set-up and make sure it works properly."

"Your wish is my command."

"So who's going to be Santa Claus?" Hannah asked.

Brent shot her a look, which she returned with one of her own.

"At first I hadn't given it any thought, but Colleen asked me the same thing." Leslie seemed to be looking at him hopefully.

No. Way. Making it snow was one thing, but showing up at a society function as Santa was a whole other story. "What about your brother? We can call him St. Nick."

Hannah and Leslie both laughed.

"I can imagine how that would go over," Leslie said. "But I was thinking of something a little different. Santa in a red suit is fine for a children's party, but I want this to be a grown-up affair. Hors d'oeuvres, waiters circulating with champagne, that sort of thing. And although people will pay quite a bit to attend, I'm hoping they'll be even more generous once they get there and realize how important this cause is."

Brent nodded. It all sounded good to him, as long as it meant he didn't have to be the one in the red suit.

"So I'm thinking about having a couple of men in tuxedos and wearing red hats, soliciting donations, reminding people to check out the silent auction, that sort of thing." She stopped talking and looked more hopeful than ever.

Was there any way to say no to being Santa in a tux? None that he could think of. "Tell you what," he said. "If you can convince your brother to do this, I'm in, too."

Her smile would have been thanks enough, but the light kiss on his cheek sealed the deal.

Hannah was smiling, too. "Are you two ready to eat? The table in the dining room is set and this pan is ready to come out of the oven."

Leslie jumped up and grabbed a pair of oven mitts off the counter. "Let me get it," she said. "That pan is too heavy for you to lift."

The dinner was amazing. Boeuf bourguignon turned out to be a gourmet beef stew that Hannah served with mashed potatoes and a salad and a loaf of French bread. Leslie poured glasses of red wine for herself and him, and iced tea for Hannah, and they toasted Hannah's visit and the success of Leslie's fund-raising event.

After dinner Leslie insisted that the elderly woman go to her room and rest while they cleared away the dinner dishes. When they finished that, she walked with him to the front door.

He picked up his jacket and put it on. "Thanks for dinner."

"Thanks for bringing the dress."

A few seconds ticked by and they were on the verge of an awkward silence when he remembered his gift.

"I almost forgot. I have something for you." He pulled the package from his pocket and handed it to her.

She accepted, a little reluctantly it seemed to him. "What's this for?"

"The shoes. I tried to get you another pair but they were all out of your size."

"I'm glad. I didn't want another pair, and…" She hesitated. "They were very expensive. I'm glad you didn't waste your money on them."

He instantly regretted spending anything at all.

She untied the ribbon and lifted the lid of the little box.

What if she hated this, or thought it was silly and sentimental?

"Brent, this is beautiful. It's like Cinderella's glass slipper."

The dainty high-heeled crystal shoe had been on display

in the jewelry-store window. It hadn't been the only thing he'd bought while he was there, but for now it was all he could give her.

She put it back in the box and set it on the hall table. "I love it. Thank you."

"I should go."

"In a minute. I have something for you, too." She wound her arms around his neck and brushed his mouth with hers, lightly at first and then with more purpose.

He held her and let her take control of the kiss while he ran his hands down her back, pulling her close. He felt his body respond and he could have sworn hers did, too. But he forced his hands to stop at her waist and reminded himself it was a goodnight kiss, not a let's-spend-the-night-together kiss.

He ran his hands up her sides and gently pushed her away from him. Stopping the kiss was a lot harder.

"That was me saying thank you."

"This is me saying good night." He kissed the tip of her nose. "Sleep well."

Chapter Eleven

The next day, after a late lunch, Hannah helped clear away the dishes and Leslie couldn't help noticing how tired she looked. The woman had been through a lot in the past month. Losing her home, ending up in a shelter.

"I can take care of this," Leslie said. "You should sit and put your feet up. Maybe you'd like some tea?"

"I can't have you looking after me. It wouldn't be right."

"Of course it would. You looked after me for years."

"Looking after your family was my job."

"Yes, but now we're friends. And friends let friends help each other."

"A person might think you were a lawyer, the way you lay out your arguments."

"Good. Now you go sit. Better yet, why don't you go lie down for a while? I'll bring you a cup of tea and some magazines."

"That does sound mighty good."

Leslie filled the kettle and turned it on. "Off you go, then. I'll be right there."

She watched Hannah slowly make her way down the hallway. As she laid out a tea tray, Leslie wondered what Hannah's reaction would be if she suggested making an appointment for her to see her doctor. Since the older woman made a fuss about sitting down and being waited on, Leslie decided this wasn't the time to broach that subject.

While she waited for the kettle to boil, she went into the den to look for some magazines. She chose several that she thought Hannah might like. On her way out of the room, she spotted the box of stuff that belonged to Gerald. The negative energy was almost tangible. It was time to get this stuff out of here.

She took the magazines into the kitchen, set them on the tray, filled the teapot and carried it into the guest room. Hannah had slipped off her shoes and was reclining on the bed, watching *Dr. Phil*.

"You look comfortable." Leslie positioned the tray over Hannah's lap and gave her a kiss on the cheek.

"I am. And watching this show makes me count my blessings. A lot of people out there are a lot worse off than I am."

Leslie smiled. Hannah had always been as solid as a rock and more sensible than anyone she knew. "Can I get you anything else?"

"No, my dear. You've already done enough."

"What about a blanket?"

"Well, now that you mention it, a blanket would be nice."

Leslie took a blanket from the closet and covered the woman's legs. "Rest as long as you like. I need to take care of a few things this afternoon."

Hannah patted her hand. "Thank you. Run along and have a good time. Maybe spend some time with that nice young man who was here last night."

"Brent? Um, I think he's working." Not that it hadn't crossed her mind. Since he worked for her brother and she was now planning the fund-raiser, she could easily come up with a reason to drop by the house they were renovating to ask Nick for a favor.

Come to think of it…

No.

First things first.

This afternoon she needed to get her former fiancé out of her life, once and for all. Then she could think about moving on.

She poured Hannah's tea and set the pot back on the tray and the tray on the nightstand. "Have a good rest. I'll check in on you later."

She went back down the hallway to the den, closed the door and dialed Gerald's number. He answered and although he sounded surprised to hear from her, he agreed, somewhat reluctantly she thought, to come by and pick up his things.

While she waited, she took the box out of the closet and put it by the front door, then she wandered restlessly through the house. What had possessed her to buy such a big place? A little house like Brent's was all she needed. But she knew why she'd bought this one. It had several bedrooms, a family room and a den, and a nice little enclosed patio. She'd thought it would be a perfect place to raise a family. She and Gerald had never actually talked about a family—she'd just assumed he'd want one. Everyone did, right? And it had been the last thing she'd needed to cross off her stupid list.

The doorbell finally rang, twenty minutes past the time he said he'd be there. So typical. For a few seconds, she stood with her hand on the doorknob. How would it feel to see him again?

There was only one way to find out.

She opened the door and felt…nothing. Not a damn thing. She tried to whip up some anger, but even that wouldn't come. So she calmly stood there, waiting for him to say something. Her composure seemed to unravel his.

He looked even paler than usual, as though he hadn't been sleeping well. And was his hair already starting to thin? It was as if she was seeing him for the first time, and she had to wonder what the hell she'd been thinking. He shifted his weight from one foot to the other, back and forth, and finally stammered out a greeting. "It's good to see you, Leslie. I've been waiting for you to call. We need to talk."

You were waiting for *me* to call? *Give me a break.*

He stepped forward and attempted to put his arms around her.

She quickly moved out of range and, with one foot, slid the box toward him. "I don't want to talk. I want you to get your things out of my house."

"Come on, Leslie. You're not being reasonable."

Now she was angry. "I'm not the one who had my tongue in somebody else's mouth on our wedding day."

"Candice was just—"

"Horny?"

He was plainly shocked. "That was tacky."

"And feeling up one of my bridesmaids wasn't?"

"It didn't mean anything. You know what she's like."

"I don't care what *she's* like. This isn't about her, it's about *you*. You're the one who was getting married. I'm not upset with Candice." Much. "You're the one who was supposed to be committed to our relationship. Maybe I should be grateful that Candice showed me that's not possible."

Instead of looking cowed, he tried a different approach. "So, where were you for the past couple of days?"

How dare he ask a question like that? But at least she knew that information hadn't spread around town. She certainly didn't want Brent's name to be dragged through the mud with hers. "I was staying with a friend."

"We checked with your friends. They were all looking for you."

Leslie smiled smugly. "Looks like you're not the only one who has secrets."

"You're telling me—"

"I'm not telling you anything. Where and with whom I

stayed is none of your damn business. I want you to take your things and get the hell out of my life."

"Come on, Leslie. This isn't like you."

Oh my God, she thought. Did he really think she'd overlook his indiscretions and stay with him? Of course he did. Her mother did. All her life she'd done what everyone else expected of her, never what she wanted. Did she even know what she wanted?

Yes, she did.

"You know something, Gerald? This is *exactly* like me. I wanted a faithful husband and a perfect marriage and—" She paused and took a long breath to steady herself. *Someone who actually loves me.* "I thought you could give me those things. I was wrong. Now please leave."

That seemed to convince him. He picked up the box but gave her one last pleading look. "You're sure there's nothing I can do to change your mind?"

"I'm sure," she said, firmly and with emphasis. "You won't want to leave that box lying around. Your ring and the jewelry are in there."

His face fell. "You should keep them."

"I can't." She stepped back and closed the door.

She went into the kitchen and looked around. For once, she wished she was the dramatic type who could smash plates against the wall, or scream at the top of her lungs or…

Not only was she not the dramatic type, she couldn't think of anything else outrageous to do. Pathetic. She needed to talk to someone, though.

Her mother was out of the question. Nick? Her friends? No.

Brent. That's who she wanted to talk to. Because he wouldn't just talk, he would put his arms around her and make her feel that everything was okay. And although that wouldn't be altogether fair to him, she really needed to feel okay. Would he mind? She didn't think he would.

Without giving herself time to talk herself out of it, she left a note on the counter for Hannah, grabbed her handbag and keys and left.

BRENT'S TRUCK was parked in the driveway, which meant he had to be home from work. She pulled in behind it and debated the wisdom of coming here. If she left now, Brent would be none the wiser and she wouldn't be on the verge of doing something she'd regret.

Max appeared in the living room window, front paws on the sill.

So much for changing her mind.

Brent and his dog met her at the front door. Max's unabandoned exuberance offset Brent's apparent lack of enthusiasm at seeing her there.

"Hi," he said. "I wasn't expecting to see you." His hair was still damp from the shower and he was barefoot, which meant he'd only been home long enough to shower and change into clean jeans and a white T-shirt. "Max, quiet!"

The barking stopped but Brent held on to the dog's collar to prevent him from lunging at Leslie.

"I wasn't sure if I should come here."

"You're welcome here anytime, you know that. Come on in, before Max gives himself a coronary."

She stepped inside the now familiar little house and immediately felt that this was the right place to be. "Thanks," she said, unable to keep the tremor out of her voice.

"What's wrong?"

"Gerald came to my place this afternoon."

"I see," he said quietly. "I think you'd better sit down." He led her to the sofa and waited till she was seated before he joined her.

The dog ran into the kitchen and dashed back with his teddy bear in his mouth. "Not now, Max."

"He's fine," she said. "He puts things into perspective."

"What did Gerald want?" he asked.

"Actually, I called him. I wanted him to get his things out of my town house. But you were right. He wanted to talk about getting back together."

"What did you tell him?"

"What do think I told him? No way. And then I told him to take his stuff and get the hell out of my life."

Brent's eyebrows shot up.

"You don't have to look so surprised. I know how to tell somebody to go to hell."

"Yeah, you're a total bad ass."

"Don't make fun of me."

Brent took her hands in his. "Then don't make it so easy."

She wanted to put her arms around him and thank him for being so understanding.

He wanted details. "What did Gerald say when you told him to get lost?"

"He blamed it all on Candice. Can you believe that? Like he had nothing to do with it."

"I'm sorry."

"That's not the worst of it. He tried to tell me that I was overreacting, and then he wanted to know where I'd been for two days. As if that was any of his business."

"Did you tell him?"

"No, of course not."

He looked a little disappointed.

"After he cleared out, I was so mad I wanted to smash something. Hannah was resting and I didn't want her to see me like this. I didn't know what else to do…"

"So you came here."

"Do you mind? I can't talk to my family or to Allison about this. Not yet."

"I don't mind at all."

Max sat on the floor in front of her and dropped his teddy bear in her lap. She ran her shaky fingers through the dog's shaggy fur. "I missed you."

"Just him?" Brent asked.

Images from the two days she'd spent with him flashed through her mind. The way he'd carried her into the house, unzipped her wedding gown, retrieved her ring from the plumbing, kissed her. Especially the way he'd kissed her, and the way he'd backed off when she'd said she wasn't ready to make love. A little voice in her head was telling her that she was ready now.

"I missed you, too," she said.

"But we saw each other last night," he reminded her.

"That's not what I'm talking about."

"What are you talking about?"

"This." She ran her hands up his hard-muscled arms and along his shoulders.

He didn't pull away, and that gave her the courage to initiate a kiss. He backed off before her lips touched his.

"What are you doing?" he asked.

"Picking up where we left off last night."

"That was a good-night kiss. I'm not sure what this is."

"Isn't it obvious?"

"What's obvious is that you had a run-in with your ex. You're upset, so you came here. Being here with me like this might seem like a good idea right now, but it might not seem that way afterward."

Was he turning her down? "I'll bet I'm not the first woman to do this."

"What does that have to do with anything?"

"Did you turn down the others?"

His head moved slowly from side to side.

"Then why are you saying no to me?"

"Because you're different, Leslie. Don't you get it? I've wanted to make love to you for as long as I can remember."

That's why she was here. A moment ago she couldn't have articulated it, but she wanted to be made love to by someone who loved her. "I know," she said.

He shook his head, firmly this time. "Don't ask me to be your booty call."

"What?"

"Don't get all high and mighty with me. That's exactly what you're here for, and it's not going to happen."

Oh. God. This would be a good time for the ground to open up and swallow her alive. She had never done anything like this, and the outcome was the exact opposite of what she'd expected it to be. They were sitting side by side on the sofa with his thigh pressed against hers, and her hands on his arms, and she had no idea how to gracefully extract herself from this ridiculous situation.

Since when did men turn down women who offered to sleep with them? Gerald certainly hadn't been capable of it.

But she already knew that Brent wasn't like most men.

He must have sensed her discomfort. "I meant what I said the other night. When you're ready for this, I'll be waiting."

"My wanting to be with you isn't enough?"

"No."

"Why?"

"Because it won't be enough for you."

She pulled her hands away and folded them in her lap. Did she dare tell him the truth? How could she not? "Gerald was…is…the only man I've ever been with. He didn't care about me, not really. I need to know the difference."

She couldn't bring herself to look at him, and he didn't answer. He took her hand and silently led her into his bedroom.

Chapter Twelve

They stood next to his bed, and he kissed her. "You're sure about this?" he asked.

"Completely sure."

And apparently willing to let him take charge. Through the haze that was already clouding his mind, a vague thought crystallized. A man who cheated on his bride on the morning of the wedding was too selfish to be a good lover.

Leslie might not know the difference between having sex and being made love to, yet. That was something he could show her, and he might never have another chance.

He helped her onto the bed and crawled on next to her. She was so amazingly beautiful, he found it hard to believe that aside from her ex, no one had managed to seduce her, although he was sure others had tried.

He kissed her and then lifted his head so he could look into her eyes while he touched her. When he kissed her again, he slipped his hand under her shirt. Her breathing was already quicker, pressing her hard nipple into his palm every time she inhaled.

She tried to deepen the kiss but he held back. "Slow down," he whispered against her lips. "There's no hurry."

"What if I change my mind again?"

If her reaction to him stroking a nipple through her bra was anything to go by, he wasn't taking much of a gamble. She was already aroused, and he had barely started. "I'll take my chances," he said.

Her clothes melted away, item by item, until every square inch of her body was exposed to him. Her hands roamed under his shirt and he finally stripped it away so she could touch him, too, but he stopped at that. For now this was about her, and he didn't ask her what she wanted, he showed her.

He let her reactions guide him and when he felt she was near the edge, he let her kiss him. It was a deep, passionate kiss that damn near sucked the old life out of him, until her little gasps of pleasure had him feeling like a completely new man.

She moved closer and touched him through his jeans. "I think it's your turn."

He shook his head. "No, I'm pretty sure it's still yours." But he moved off the bed, grabbed a condom from a drawer in the nightstand and had his jeans and underwear off and the condom on in record time.

Leslie lay tangled in his sheets, her skin glowing with the pink flush of orgasm. Her eyes widened as her gaze took in his erection.

It was the wrong time to be thinking that Gerald Bedford must not measure up, but he thought it just the same. Then he moved onto the bed and over her, and she opened her legs to let him in, and the two of them were the only people on his mind.

He lowered himself into her, slowly, agonizingly slowly, giving her time to adjust to him being there, all the while thinking that the excruciating pleasure of being inside her might actually kill him. And then she gave herself to him, and he prayed for enough control to please her again. He wove his fingers between hers and raised her hands above her head, holding her there while she strained against him. He stayed with her, persuading one tremor after another from her, before he let himself go.

When he finally managed to open his eyes, she was looking

at him. And her eyes were telling him that she had the answer to her question.

"I've wanted this forever," he said.

"I think maybe I have, too. It just took me longer to figure it out."

"Will you spend the night?"

"I can't. I left a note for Hannah, telling her I'd be back in a few hours. I don't want her to worry."

"You could call her."

"I really need to go, Brent. But I'd like to see you again. Soon."

"Will tomorrow be too soon?"

She laughed. "Maybe not soon enough."

"We could go out for dinner, or maybe see a movie."

She hesitated. "I don't know...."

"Don't get me wrong. I can't think of a better way than this to spend time with you. I just don't want you to think this is the only thing I'm interested in."

He lay back against the pillows and drew her into the circle of his arms.

He wanted to tell her he loved her. Then he wanted to track down Gerald Bedford and gloat.

Under the circumstances, neither was appropriate. He ran a hand over the soft, smooth skin of her belly, thinking another orgasm might be. He congratulated himself on having such good instincts.

"Brent, if you keep doing that, I won't be able to leave."

"So my plan is working?"

She didn't say anything, which led him to believe it was the perfect plan.

Oh, yes. There we go. Perfect.

"I've never done this before," she said breathlessly.

"You've never used a man for sex?"

"That's not what I meant."

He kissed her. "What haven't you done before?" he asked.

"Had three orgasms in—" She twisted to look at the clock on the nightstand. "An hour? Is that even possible?"

"Apparently." And all of a sudden it was okay that someone else had been her first because he intended to be her last.

THE NEXT AFTERNOON Leslie drove past Donaldson's Deli and found a parking spot at the end of the block. She'd called Allison to ask her about helping with the fund-raiser and they had agreed to meet at their favorite coffee spot. She checked her makeup in the rearview mirror, tucked her keys into her handbag and stepped out of her car.

Four teenage boys in a convertible honked and waved as they cruised by. She smiled and thought, eat your hearts out, boys.

A week ago, that thought would have surprised her. Today she felt undeniably sexy, and it was all thanks to Brent Borden. She walked down the block with more swing in her step than she'd felt in a long time.

The sidewalk was crowded with shoppers and tourists, and she hoped Allison had already arrived and found a table. She was looking forward to getting her friend involved in the fund-raiser. Because there were two things about Allison that she knew for certain. She loved parties, and absolutely no one could say no to her—so she was counting on her best friend to take on the silent auction.

She pushed open the door of the deli and gave old Mr. Donaldson a quick wave before she spotted Allison sitting at the corner table. As always, her friend looked more like a cover model than the mother of two children.

Allison quickly stood up and hugged her. "I'm *so* glad we could sit down for a real gabfest."

Leslie hugged her back, and they took their seats together. "Me, too. Did you just get your hair cut? I like it short. It suits you."

"Isn't it great? Maggie suggested it." Then her friend lowered her voice to a whisper. "How are you holding up? I still can't believe what Gerald did. And with Candice, of all people."

Mr. Donaldson approached their table and peered over the top of his bifocals. "Afternoon, ladies. What can I bring you?"

"I'll have a cappuccino," Allison said.

Leslie smiled at him. "I think I'll have an iced coffee. And a biscotti."

"Oooh, iced coffee sounds wonderful. I'll have one of those instead."

"Would you like something to go with that?" he asked.

Allison shook her head. "No, thanks." Which meant she was counting calories, as usual.

As soon as he was out of hearing, Leslie leaned toward her friend. "So, how did you find out about them?"

"How does anyone find out anything in this town? Turns out that their little indiscretion wasn't all that discreet."

"I'll say. Even *I* saw them together."

Allison put an arm around her shoulders and gave an affectionate squeeze. "Sweetie, I'm so sorry this happened but I have to say, you look fantastic. The second you walked through the door, I was wondering, what's her secret?"

Sex? Even Allison, with her flare for the dramatic, would be shocked to hear her say that. "Honestly, I feel more relieved than anything. I mean, what was I thinking? Gerald and I didn't love each other." Admitting she'd been that shallow wasn't easy, but she was coming to terms with it. "And imagine what a disaster this could have been if I hadn't found out until after the wedding."

"So what are your plans? Will you go back to work right away?"

She hesitated until she decided how much she needed to tell her friend. "That's one of the things I want to talk about. I'd arranged for a month off and I've decided to take it. Do you remember Hannah Greene? My mother's housekeeper?"

"I do. She used to make all those fabulous pastries. Does she still work for her?"

"Oh, no. Not for quite a few years, but she recently had to move out of her apartment and hasn't been able to find another one. I've invited her to stay with me."

"And that's okay with you?"

"It's more than okay. She insists it's temporary, until she finds another place to live, but I'm enjoying her company. I hope she'll stay for a while." Even though it was going to affect how much time she and Brent could spend together.

"Is that who you've been staying with since Saturday?"

"No. It was just this weekend that I discovered she was living at the homeless shelter."

Allison was more shocked than Leslie would have expected her to be. "Oh my God. Please tell me *you* didn't spend the weekend at the shelter."

Stunned, Leslie sat back in her chair and stared at Allison. How could she even think that? "Of course not. I would have gone back to my place and risked having a run-in with Gerald and my mother before I'd do something like that."

"Well, that's a relief."

For heaven's sake, Leslie thought. She loved her friend dearly but to be honest, she could be a little on the dense side.

Mr. Donaldson arrived with their drinks and set the tall, frosty glasses on the table. After he put down the plate with Leslie's biscotti, he hovered a moment. "You wanted chocolate, didn't you?"

"That's right."

He had been running the deli since before Leslie and Allison were born. If anyone had a finger on the pulse of this town, he did, right down to remembering his customers' favorite flavor of biscotti and their preference of sandwiches. "So," he said. "I hear Hannah Greene's staying with you."

"Yes, isn't that wonderful?"

"It surely is," he said. "Funny, isn't it, how things always have a way of working themselves out for the best?"

"Yes, it is." She knew he wasn't just talking about Hannah, and she appreciated his roundabout way of offering support.

"You ladies enjoy your coffee. And good luck with that project of yours."

"You have a project?" Allison asked as he returned to his station behind the counter.

"That's really what I wanted to talk to you about."

While they sipped their iced coffee, Leslie outlined her ideas for the fund-raiser. Allison listened with moderate interest until she realized it would be a gala event at the Durrance estate.

"I dropped into Jocelyn Cartwright's boutique yesterday and saw the perfect dress."

Leslie sighed. Allison's motivation was less than ideal but if it took a new dress to get her on board, so be it. She needed her help.

"That's great," she said. "There's just one more thing." She explained the need for keeping the location a secret until the publicity had been taken care of.

"Deceiving your mother? My, aren't we living dangerously these days," Allison said.

Yes, I am, Leslie thought. And you don't know the half of it.

"So you haven't told me how you ended up being involved in this. Or where you were for two days. We looked all over town for you. I was worried sick."

"You shouldn't have been. I was staying with a friend."

"Ah, in case you've forgotten, your friends are my friends, too. You weren't with any of them. Trust me, we checked." Sooner or later Allison was going to find out, and she wouldn't stop asking questions until she did.

Leslie took a deep breath before taking the plunge. "I was at Brent's place."

Allison's finely penciled eyebrows arched in disbelief. "Brent Borden?" But even as she asked the question, her mouth was slowly forming a sly smile. "Does Gerald know?"

"It's none of his business. Nick is the only one who knows. He and Maggie, that is. And Brent's mother. Oh, and Hannah."

Allison rolled her eyes. "Oh well, then it's a state secret."

"None of those people are going to gossip, and I'd appreciate it if you could keep it to yourself. It's nobody else's business, and I don't want to drag Brent into this."

Allison's smile hinted at conspiracy. "I could be persuaded to keep your secret, but I need details! How did you end up with him?"

"It was pouring rain when I left the church. I had to get out of there, but I had no idea where I was going. He happened to be driving by, and he gave me a lift. I didn't have my keys or anything with me and I didn't want to go home anyway, so he took me to his place."

"He 'happened to be driving by' the morning of your wedding. Now there's a coincidence."

In spite of Allison's sarcasm, Leslie smiled. "He told me why he was there. It was no coincidence."

"It's so obvious that he's still totally in love with you, and you spent…what?…two or three days with him? That must have been awkward."

"Not really. He was very sweet. He went out and got clothes for me. He even bought me a toothbrush."

Allison was looking at her intently. "If I didn't know you better, I might think *you* were falling for *him*."

Leslie felt a flush spread across her face and hoped that her makeup would keep it hidden. Apparently not.

"You are!" Allison said.

"We're friends."

"Did you sleep with him?"

The warm flush turned into a heat wave.

"Oh. My. God. Leslie! I would so love to rub Gerald's nose in that juicy bit of information."

"No! Allison, you have to promise you won't do that. I don't want people gossiping about Brent."

Allison leaned forward and gave her a wink. "So, how was he?"

"I'm not going to answer that!"

"I think you just did." Allison leaned on her elbows and smiled suggestively. "So that's your secret for looking like a million dollars."

Leslie wished she could think of some way to change the subject, but she knew Allison well enough to know that wasn't going to happen.

"After all these years he has to be pretty happy about this, but how are you going to get rid of him?"

Leslie lowered her gaze. How could Allison ask a question like that? Did she really think she'd sleep with someone she didn't want to be with?

"Leslie? You *can't* be serious." Allison pushed her glass toward the middle of the table.

"I…I don't know. He's actually very smart and funny and—"

"Hot."

Leslie smiled. "Yes, he is."

"Does Nick know?"

"Only if Brent tells him, but I don't think he will."

"You know it's only a matter of time before Gerald finds out."

"Since you're the only person who knows, I'm sure he won't."

Allison did a finger twist over her closed lips and pretended to throw away a key.

As much as Leslie wanted to believe her secret was safe, she knew the odds were against her. "I want you to know nothing happened between us while I was staying with him. After I went home, I packed up Gerald's things and gave everything back."

"Even that beautiful ring?"

"Especially the ring. Why would I want to keep it?"

"I'd have been tempted."

Leslie had been tempted to let it make its way to the sewer, but Allison didn't need to know about that. She glanced around to make sure no one was listening. "And I never would have…you know, with Brent…until I'd ended things with Gerald."

Allison shrugged. "You were worried about *his* feelings?"

Not even remotely. "No, just Brent's."

"I see. Can I ask one more thing?"

Why not?

"If you were staying with Brent, how did you find out about Hannah and get involved in this fund-raising project?"

She gave as brief an explanation as possible about the work Brent's mother was doing at the shelter.

Allison heaved a dramatic sigh. "I'm not even going ask how his mother factors into this. I just hope you know what you're doing."

Leslie glanced at her watch. "Thanks for saying you'll help with the thing for the shelter. I have to run, but I'll be in touch." Brent was coming over and she had just enough time to pick up groceries and start on dinner before he arrived.

Chapter Thirteen

Brent walked through the Durrance estate with Leslie while she checked the party preparations one last time and crossed items off her checklist. The past few weeks had raced by in a flurry of preparations for the Christmas in July party and as many stolen hours with Leslie as the two of them could manage. He could hardly believe she'd pulled this together in such a short time. Even his mother was impressed, and that was no small feat. At least not where Leslie was concerned, and now it was more important than ever that the two of them get along.

A technician was on the stage doing a sound check and his voice boomed from hidden spots in the shrubs and flower beds. Caterers were setting up steam trays on long, white-draped tables. A woman in a navy business suit waved to them from across the lawn. "Leslie? Can you come over here and confirm the location of the cashier's booth?"

Leslie waved back. "Do you mind doing this now?" she asked Brent. "It should only take a couple of minutes and once that's done, we can finish going through the list."

"You're the boss," he said. Any delay was fine with him. It meant they could spend more time together, and it gave him an opportunity to figure out how to ask her...

"I am not your boss."

"And yet I've spent the last two weeks doing everything you asked me to."

"I didn't mention that I would make it worth your while?"

"First I've heard of it. What do you have in mind?"

Her smile was answer enough. At least for now.

To say the past couple of weeks had been incredible would be the understatement of a lifetime. He hadn't wanted to scare her off with the *L*-word, especially since she'd been hinting that her interest in him had gone way beyond the physical, but he'd done everything he could think of to show her how much he loved her.

They were still keeping their relationship under wraps, although Hannah knew what was going on and seemed to approve. If his mother suspected anything, she would have said something by now. Nick hadn't clued in, but then he was totally preoccupied with the woman in his life. Right now the only thing Brent wanted was for Leslie to take the final step and go public with him, and tonight seemed like the perfect time to do it. He wanted to go to this party with her, as a couple, and he had a feeling she was ready to do that.

They finished with the bookkeeper and carried on with Leslie's checklist.

"Do you think we have enough tables and chairs?" she asked.

"Everything," he answered, "including you, looks perfect."

She was wearing a sleeveless yellow dress with a V-neck that provided the occasional glimpse of soft curves and something lacy. And if he leaned closer, under the pretext of looking at the list on her clipboard…oh, yeah. Very nice.

"The lights on the tree have been checked, right?" She glanced up at him, waiting for his answer, and then narrowed her eyes.

"What?"

"Were you looking down the front of my dress?"

"Me? No. Nooo."

"We're almost finished. I need you to pay attention to what we're doing."

"I'm paying attention."

"You were? Then why don't you answer my question?"

"There was a question?"

She rolled her eyes at him. "I asked if you've checked the lights. The tree-lighting ceremony will be one of the highlights of the evening. It has to be perfect."

"Yes, I checked the lights. I checked the lights on the tree, the lights on all the shrubs, the lights around the fountain, the lights on the podium. When this place is lit up, even the people on the space station will be impressed."

"Very funny."

He draped an arm around her shoulders and looked down at her list again.

She shot him a look. "Would you behave?"

"I am."

"Oh, please," she said, but she was laughing and he loved the sound of it. "You couldn't behave if your life depended on it."

He made the Scout's honor sign. "I was looking at your list." Which was the truth this time, and he was relieved to see the only thing left on it was the snow-making machine. He took the pencil from between her fingers and checked it off. "There. We're done. And tonight I'll be on my best behavior. That's a promise. But right now…" They had reached the back of the grounds, far away from the commotion of the set-up crews.

He steered her into a vine-covered gazebo and put his arms around her. "Right now I need to ask you something." But first he wanted to kiss her. *Had to* was more like it.

And she kissed him back. Everything she did—the playful swirl of her tongue against his, the flirty little way she moved her body—left him breathless and wanting more. And when she drew one knee up the inside of his thigh, even he knew it was time to slow down.

"Ms. Durrance. Trying to seduce me out here in your mother's gazebo? I'm shocked."

"My mother is gone for the day. Her nose is still out of joint because I swindled her into hosting the party, although she has grudgingly acknowledged that the fund-raiser will be a success. She'll be here tonight but she refuses to help, and that's fine with me. I'd rather she didn't interfere."

"Me, too. Besides, I'm scared to death of your mother." He kissed her again, and she kissed him back. "But I assume it's okay if this army of volunteers catches us making out."

Leslie pulled away, laughing. "No, it's most definitely not. And while we're on the subject of scary mothers…"

"Ah, yes. The formidable Colleen Borden."

"She is that, but I think she's coming around. When I showed her the profit projections, she seemed impressed. And grateful."

"She should be."

Even through the thin fabric of her dress and her latest bit of lace temptation, he felt Leslie's nipple respond, and then he felt her little moan against his mouth and he didn't know how either of them could put a stop to this.

But he did have a question to ask her, and something to give to her. He'd been trying to build up his courage all week, and he didn't know when a better opportunity would present itself.

He unwound her arms from his neck and took her hands in his. Her eyes had taken on that passion-induced dreamy quality that he had come to know over the past few weeks, and wanted to keep seeing. Forever.

"Let's sit down for a little bit," he said.

She settled onto a bench beside him, but not without protest. "I still need to check with the caterers—"

"This will just take a minute."

She gazed up at him, suddenly wary. "Is something wrong?"

"No, everything's fine." Or would be, if he could breathe. "Brent?"

"I know this might seem kind of soon, but—" He paused and dug into the pocket of his jeans. "I wanted to give you this." He held up the ring with the rose quartz stone. "And ask you—"

Surprise registered on her face. Or was it alarm? Damn. He was going about this all wrong. She deserved a romantic proposal, one that was written across the sky. Should he get down on one knee? No, that wasn't his style. Somehow he didn't think it was hers, either.

"I'm asking you to marry me."

She stared at him.

Oh, man. This had been a bad idea.

"Leslie?"

She blinked. "I'm just… I wasn't expecting this."

"But you had to know that I'm in love with you?"

She nodded. "It's just that it's only been a few weeks and…I don't know what to say."

Clearly, she wasn't going to say yes. "Can you think about it?" he asked.

She smiled then. Just a small one, but it gave him a shred of hope. "You know I can't say yes, Brent. Not yet. It's too soon. But I'm not saying no, either," she added quickly. She held out her right hand.

She wasn't saying no, and she was going to let him put the ring onto her finger. On her right hand. Which was better than no hand at all. He slid the ring into place. "If it's not the right size, I can take it back and—"

But she was shaking her head. "It's fine. I love it, I really do, and I want to keep it. I'll take it in next week to be sized."

"Are you sure?"

"I'm sure." She leaned close and kissed him lightly.

It wasn't the biggest or most expensive ring he could have given her, and he found himself wanting to explain why he'd chosen it. And he wanted to ask how long it might be before "not saying no" might turn into yes. But he couldn't ask.

She held out her hand and gazed at the ring. "I really do love this." Even without looking at him, it was as though she could read his mind. "It feels like you chose it especially for me."

Those words kick-started his heart. He had hardly dared to hope that she would understand why he'd chosen this ring, but she did. "I love you," he said.

At first she didn't say anything. When she did, the response came too slowly for it to be what he wanted to hear.

"Don't." Gently, he touched a finger to her lips. "I can wait."

"Thank you. Can we keep this to ourselves for a while?"

"So I should cancel the full-page ad in the *New York Times?*"

She laughed, and it helped them both relax. She had accepted the ring, and she hadn't said no. He didn't want to wait. Hell, he'd wanted the world to hear about it tonight, but he would wait. Forever, if that's what it took.

He stood and held out a hand to her.

She took it. "We should get back to work. After I check with the caterers, I have to go home and get ready."

"You're not doing that here?"

"No, it's easier to go home than to bring everything I need over here. Besides, Hannah is coming with me."

They hadn't talked about whether they would arrive separately or together. He asked before his courage failed him. "Do the two of you need an escort for this evening?"

She gave him a long look, probably working up to telling him that she wasn't ready for the two of them to be seen together in public.

"I'll drive over with her in my car."

It wasn't the response he'd hoped for, but he wouldn't force the issue. "That's fine," he said. "I'll meet you back here."

LESLIE TOWELED herself dry and rubbed lotion onto her arms and legs. She went into her bedroom and put on the bra and panties she'd laid out on the bed. They were pink silk and, hands down, Brent's favorites. She had never imagined that shopping for lingerie with a certain man in mind could be so much fun. She opened her jewelry box and while she debated what to wear with her dress, the sparkle of Brent's ring caught her eye. She picked it up and slid it onto her right hand. Then she took the ring off and tried it on her left hand. He'd been disappointed that she hadn't accepted his proposal, but she would. When the time was right.

She went back into the bathroom and squirted some moisturizer into the palm of her hand.

The strange thing, she thought as she smoothed it onto her face, was how easy it was for her to imagine herself living in Brent's house, taking his dog for a walk, cooking dinner for him, making love. That sounded a lot like marriage.

Which she'd been telling herself she wasn't ready for. It was too soon after Gerald. She couldn't begin to imagine what people would say if she announced…

"Stop it," she said to her reflection. "That sounds like something your mother would say."

But she couldn't help it. She did care what people thought about her. Old habits were difficult to overcome. It didn't hurt to daydream about it. Maybe Brent would move in here. No, Max needed a yard. She would move to Brent's place and they'd leave Hannah here.

Actually, that wasn't a bad idea. The hard part would be convincing Hannah to go along with it.

She rinsed her hands and reached for a towel. The ring slipped off her finger and skittered across the marble vanity.

"No!" She slapped her hand over it as it rolled toward the sink.

She stood there, frozen. She would never have been able to explain to Brent how *his* ring had ended up down the drain.

And he had been right, of course. The ring needed to be sized and until it had been, she didn't dare wear it and risk losing it. She took it back into her bedroom and set it safely inside the jeweler's box.

When she finished dressing, she went downstairs and found Hannah waiting in the kitchen.

"You look lovely. You'll be the belle of the ball," Leslie said.

"It's the most beautiful dress I've ever worn," Hannah said. "But I'd be happier not knowing how much you paid for it."

"Tonight is my gift to you, remember? No worries about money, and no more protesting." Leslie thought the robin's-egg-blue dress and matching coat suited Hannah perfectly. If this were a wedding, she could pass for mother of the bride.

"Is Brent coming to pick us up?" she asked.

"No. I thought it would be easier for us to take my car. This way we don't have to wait for him."

Apparently Hannah saw right through that, and she didn't mind saying so. "He's always been punctual," she said. "There's a lot to be said for punctuality."

As far as Hannah was concerned there was a lot to be said for all of Brent's qualities.

"You're right, he is. But we should go, or we'll be late."

"Humph," was all Hannah said as she followed her out to the car.

Chapter Fourteen

Although Brent had arrived early, the Durrance estate was already buzzing with activity when a kid in a reflective safety vest directed him into a parking spot. Leslie's car was already there, which meant she hadn't wasted any time getting ready and getting back here. He picked up a florist's box off the passenger seat and tossed his keys under the floor mat. He didn't want to carry them in his pocket. And given the luxury cars that were already starting to arrive, his truck was the last thing anyone would want to steal.

He headed for the grounds and immediately spotted Leslie. He stopped walking and watched her settle Hannah at a small table on the edge of the seating area. She took his breath away.

Several days ago he'd asked Hannah to find out the color of the dress Leslie was wearing, and she'd said it was pink. But pink didn't quite describe it. Shimmery mother of pearl was more like it. The dress fitted her slender body like a glove and the thin straps and thigh-high side slit showed lots of skin. He was now intimately familiar with every inch of that skin and he'd be just as happy if no one else saw it.

He quickly reminded himself that he had no justification for feeling that way. He probably wouldn't, except that he knew Gerald Bedford III was going to be there.

Is that why Leslie had chosen the dress?

As a kind of eat-your-heart-out reminder of what the stupid jerk had given up?

Brent hated himself for even thinking it. That wasn't Leslie's style. Besides, she'd accepted the ring. She hadn't accepted his proposal, not yet, but taking his ring meant something.

He just wished he knew what.

He did his best to appear casual as he strolled across the lawn toward them. Hannah saw him first, her smile adding a few more crinkles around her eyes. Leslie turned to see what had caught the woman's attention, and she smiled, too. A slow, sexy smile that was full of promise and had him wishing the evening was already over.

"Hi," she said as he approached them. "You look amazing."

He casually slid an arm around her and kissed the top of her head.

Hannah beamed her approval, but Leslie edged away. The movement was so quick and decisive that a chance observer might not have noticed. To him, it hit like a left hook to the solar plexus.

There was no mistaking the pleading look in those brown eyes. *Can we keep this to ourselves for a while?*

He'd thought she'd meant the ring, not…everything.

He set the box on the table and lifted the lid. Nestled there in the waxy tissue paper were two orchid corsages.

"I thought Hannah would prefer something on the traditional side," he said, handing the delicate flower to Leslie. "I'll let you have the honor of pinning it on," he added. "No sense in her having to make a trip to the emergency room before we go to the party."

Hannah laughed at that, even though her eyes had become a little watery. "You foolish boy," she said. "You should not be spending your hard-earned money on flowers for an old woman."

"Old?" he asked, feigning surprise. "I was hoping you'd

be my dancing partner tonight, especially since Leslie's going to be so busy."

Leslie glanced around, as though checking to see if anyone had heard him.

So, that's how it was going to be.

Hannah waved a hand at him. "Stuff and nonsense. Everything's under control. The two of you should have left me at home and come here together."

Once the corsage was pinned to her dress, Hannah smiled. "It's too much," she said, glancing at Leslie. "Can you believe she took me shopping and bought this dress for me?"

"Tonight is my gift to you," Leslie said to her. "And you look beautiful."

"You're both beautiful," Brent said.

Leslie glanced around again.

Fine, he thought. He'd stop talking about her. About them. But he let his eyes roam freely over her slender curves. He could keep quiet for one evening, but she couldn't stop him from looking.

"This is for you," he said, lifting a wrist corsage from the box. "I didn't want to take a chance on ruining your dress." He held it for her and she slipped her hand through the loop. The front of her dress was cut low enough to make him regret not having the chance to pin something on it.

"Thank you," she said. "It's gorgeous."

"So are you." Especially given the delicate pink flush that colored her skin. He was still holding on to her hand, and that's when he noticed that the ring wasn't there. He stroked her ring finger with his thumb, and she snatched her hand away.

She shot him a warning look. "You promised me this afternoon that you would behave."

"I'm not sure it was a promise."

"Brent, please."

"Fine," he said. "Best behavior."

"Oh, I almost forgot." She handed him a red-and-white Santa hat.

"What's this for?"

"You agreed, remember?"

"Not really."

"Yes, you do. Nick and Allison's husband are the other official Santas for the evening."

"Are they?" Brent hadn't seen John Fontaine since the day he'd run into him at the pharmacy while he was buying a tooth-brush for Leslie. "How did you manage to talk Nick into this?"

"I can be very persuasive."

That she could. "So what exactly does an official Christmas in July Santa do at one of these functions?"

She tucked a packet of cards into his pocket. "Hand out these notices about the new shelter. Direct people to the silent auction table. Ask them if they've made a donation to the Helping Hands Foundation."

"Isn't the price of the ticket supposed to be a donation?"

"Most of these people can afford more. Don't be afraid to ask."

Why be afraid when he could be completely terrified?

People were streaming across the lawns, laughing and talking. He caught sight of his mother waving and walking toward him. He'd never seen her look so elegant, and he couldn't help wondering if Leslie had had a hand in helping his mother find a dress. Colleen Borden would never spend hard-earned money on anything this frivolous.

"Having fun?" his mother asked.

"Just got here."

"I saw you giving flowers to Leslie."

"Mom, don't start."

"I'm not starting anything. I can admit when I'm wrong, and I was wrong about her."

He hadn't dared to hope that his mother would have a

change of heart but the timing couldn't have been better. Should he tell her about the ring?

No, better not. Especially since Leslie wasn't wearing it. Besides, he'd promised Leslie they would keep this to themselves for now.

"I'm glad to hear you say that," he said.

"This morning she told me that she might have lined up a new location for the shelter."

That was news to him, but he wasn't surprised. "But you like her because she's a nice person, right? Not just because she's helping you out with the shelter?"

"There are lots of reasons for liking her, especially given that you've completely fallen for her again and…" She paused. "And it's pretty obvious that the feeling is mutual."

Brent was dumbfounded. "What did the two of you talk about when you were having those meetings?"

"It wasn't so much what she said as the way she said it."

His mother enjoyed this kind of thing way too much. "Are you going to tell me how she said what she said?"

"No. This is up to the two of you. I don't know how you'll reconcile your life with this," she said, waving a hand toward the Durrance mansion. "But you'll make it work."

Leslie approached them and as she smiled up at him, he searched her eyes for a hint of the mutual feelings his mother claimed were there. While he watched the two of them chatting like old friends, he caught sight of Leslie's mother strolling purposefully toward them.

He cleared his throat, and Leslie glanced up.

"Hello, Mother. I'd like you to meet Colleen Borden. She's one of the directors of the Helping Hands Foundation, and she runs the homeless shelter."

"And we are extremely grateful for your generosity," his mother said. "And Leslie's, of course."

"My pleasure," Mrs. Durrance said.

Brent wasn't sure he believed her.

She settled her steely gaze on him next. Not many people intimidated him, but she had always been one of them.

"Do you remember Brent?" Leslie asked her mother. "Nick's friend?"

"I never forget people," Lydia said.

Which made Brent wonder how many things he'd done that he wished she had forgotten.

Leslie seemed anxious to end the conversation. "I'd like to introduce your mother to a few people," she said to him. "I'll catch up with you later."

He sure hoped so. For now, he supposed it was time for Santa to get to work.

LESLIE WALKED past a group of carolers in Victorian costumes, skirted the tent where the silent auction had been set up and joined Hannah and Brent's mother at the table where they had been sitting most of the evening.

"Enjoying the party?" she asked Hannah.

"I am, dear, but I think I'm on the verge of turning into a pumpkin. I think I should see about calling a taxi."

"No, I don't want you to have to do that." Leslie couldn't leave because she and Colleen would soon have to go onstage to make some closing remarks and announce how much money had been raised. Leslie had one other announcement to make, and it would be the biggest surprise of the evening.

It would be great if Hannah could stay but the poor thing was exhausted, and Leslie didn't want her to have to go into the house alone. Brent was the obvious person to drive her home but if he couldn't slip away for a few minutes, she knew Nick and Maggie would be happy to do it.

"You wait here," she said. "I'll find someone to take you home."

All evening she had hardly managed to catch a glimpse of

Brent. At first she assumed it was because he was busy and she was busy and their paths simply hadn't crossed, but now it was almost midnight and she finally had to acknowledge that he was avoiding her.

At this point she wasn't sure where to look for him. He had done a terrific job of overseeing the lighting, and the artificial snowfall had been breathtakingly beautiful. She knew he'd had reservations about being one of the evening's Santas, but apparently he'd charmed quite a few people into making significant donations. She would definitely have to thank him for that.

If she could find him.

Several of her colleagues from the law firm stopped her to congratulate her on the evening's success. She chatted briefly and as soon as she could politely extract herself from the group, she continued searching for Brent.

His disappointment at her not wearing his ring had been obvious, but they hadn't had a private moment for her to explain. She also knew it bothered him that she wouldn't say anything about it in front of their family and friends, but she wasn't ready.

What would be an acceptable length of time between calling off a wedding to one man and announcing her engagement to another? Certainly more than a couple of weeks. And she could imagine what people would say.

Gerald and Candice had come together this evening, although so far she'd managed to avoid them. She was happy to see their money put to good use for a change, but she hated that they were here. This was her night, her chance to show everyone she was not only over Gerald, but that she was a better person for it.

Finally she spotted Allison and her husband sitting at a table with a group of old friends. She waved and Allison waved back. As she threaded her way through the crowd, she smiled and politely acknowledged people as she went, but didn't let herself get caught up in any of the conversations.

"I hope you're all having a wonderful time," she said to everyone before she leaned over and whispered to Allison. "Have you seen Brent?"

"I saw him over there," she whispered back, pointing in the direction of the catering tent. "He was sitting with Nick and Maggie and a few others."

"Thanks." She stood up and smiled at everyone again, then continued to zigzag her way between the crowded tables.

She saw Nick first. He was sitting next to Maggie, with his arm around her shoulder, and he did not look happy. And then she saw Brent and knew why.

He was sitting with his back to her and Candice Bentley-Ferguson was on his lap. Her arms were loosely wrapped around his neck and his Santa hat was on her head, and Leslie wanted to throttle her.

You're more than welcome to have Gerald but this man is mine, she thought as she stormed across the remaining distance to their table.

"Well, isn't this cozy." She could hardly breathe, she was so angry. To add insult to what was already an enormous injury, Brent didn't even look guilty.

Neither did Candice, but then she probably didn't know the meaning of the word.

"I've been looking everywhere for you," Leslie said to Brent.

Before he could reply, Candice chimed in. "I've just been telling Santa what a very, very, verrry good girl I've been." She stumbled over a few words and her speech was slurred. "And he was just about to tell me what he's going to bring me for Christmas. Isn't that right, Santa?" She looked at Brent and angled her head back, trying to get her eyes to focus.

Good luck.

Brent looked far more amused than the situation merited.

"Maybe another bottle of champagne?" Leslie suggested.

"Oooh," Candice said. "There's more champagne?"

"No, there isn't. The bar is still open, though."

She giggled. "Maybe Santa would like to go with me."

Brent peeled the woman off his neck and helped her stand up and regain her balance. "Thanks," he said. "But maybe some other time."

Leslie gave him an evil look.

"Okey-dokey," Candice said and walked away, staggering slightly but at least managing to keep herself upright.

Brent folded a check in half and slipped it into his pocket. "You said you were looking for me?"

Leslie stared at him. She was furious with him for thinking he could just brush this aside, and furious with herself for being in the position of not being able to confront him about this.

"I was. Sorry for interrupting, but Hannah is getting tired and needs a ride home. I was hoping you wouldn't mind."

"Not a bit. Where is she?"

"She's sitting with your mother at one of the tables over by the pool house."

"I guess I'll see you."

He walked away, leaving her to stand and seethe. Bad enough that he was so cool and detached, but to be completely unapologetic for letting Candice hustle him? Unforgivable.

"Would you like to sit with us for a while?" Maggie asked.

Leslie swung around and looked at her and Nick. She'd forgotten she had an audience. "I'd love to, but there are still a few things left to do."

Nick was looking more relaxed, likely due to the departure of the husband-snatcher.

Maggie got up and walked around the table. Leslie was always impressed by her quirky fashion sense, and tonight's outfit was no exception. She was wearing a sleeveless emerald-green tank top over a long, dark purple silk skirt, and her dark red hair had been swept up and loosely woven with purple ribbons.

"You look really lovely tonight," Leslie said.

"Thanks. These were my aunt's pearls. I've been admiring your wrist corsage. You don't often see pink orchids."

"It's my favorite color," she said. "My…a friend gave it to me. He knows I love pink."

"He told me."

Leslie was stunned. Had Brent talked to Nick and Maggie about her? About them?

"It's okay," she said. "Nick doesn't know, and Brent didn't have to tell me. I figured it out. I have a kind of sixth sense about these things."

Leslie hugged her. "Thank you. For everything. I have an idea that you and I are going to be good friends." Maybe even sisters.

"Me, too," Maggie said. "Now you'd better go do whatever it is you have to do." She didn't say, "Follow your heart." She didn't have to.

Leslie took the shortest route possible to the table where Hannah had been sitting, but she was too late. Hannah was gone and so was Brent.

Colleen looked at her watch and stood up. "Looks as though it's speech time."

"You're right. First we should talk to the accountant to see if we can get a final tally, or at least an approximate one."

When they announced the amount of money that had been raised, the crowd applauded wildly. When Sam Beagley, the senior partner of the law firm and Leslie's father's longtime friend, announced that a new building for the shelter had been donated, Colleen actually broke down and cried. Through it all, Leslie stood onstage, wearing her best smile and graciously accepting everyone's thanks and applause. But a lot of the evening's luster had faded and she just wanted it all to be over so she could talk to Brent when he came back.

Chapter Fifteen

But Brent didn't come back and after a sleepless night, Leslie slipped out of bed at dawn and pulled on her dressing gown. The fund-raising event had surpassed even her most optimistic expectations, and she had found a new ally in Colleen Borden. Even her mother had been impressed.

Brent was the only person who didn't seem to care, and he was the one who mattered most. After proposing to her yesterday afternoon, he had been cool and withdrawn. For most of the evening he had ignored her. And if that wasn't bad enough, he had let Candice Bentley-Ferguson—the groom-stealer, of all people—flirt with him. Then he had jumped at the chance to drive Hannah home, and he hadn't bothered to return.

She didn't know what any of that meant. She didn't even know if they were still sort of engaged. She picked up the ring from where it lay next to the little pink-ribboned teddy bear and the glass slipper he'd given her and slipped it on her hand.

She looked in the mirror and held up her hand so she could admire her ring. It was the most beautiful thing anyone had ever given her. She loved it.

She loved him, and she needed to tell him that. She should have told him yesterday, and she didn't exactly know why she hadn't.

She opened her bedroom door. The house was quiet, which meant Hannah was still sleeping. Leslie made her way to the kitchen to make coffee, sliding the pocket door closed behind her so the noise wouldn't disturb Hannah.

She was filling the coffeepot with water when the ring slipped off her hand.

"No!" The pot shattered in the sink. She cranked off the tap and scanned the wreckage for her ring. "Please, please, please. You have to be here."

Frantically she slid the shards of glass around, looking for the ring, but there was no sign of it.

Blood dripped onto the broken glass. She held up her hand and tried to examine the cut on her finger but there was too much blood. Without thinking, she turned on the tap and held her finger under cold water.

"You idiot! Don't run water!" She quickly turned off the tap and stared into the sink. All the water from the coffeepot had already gone down the drain. What if it had flushed the ring out of the trap?

"Dear God, this cannot be happening."

The door slid open. "What on earth is going on in here?" Hannah asked, concern written all over her face.

"I lost the ring Brent gave me," Leslie choked out.

A smile spread across Hannah's face. "He gave you a ring?" she asked. "Where did you lose it?"

"It's down there." She pointed at the drain.

Hannah's eyes widened at the sight of the blood and broken glass. "Dear child, you're bleeding!" She quickly grabbed a towel and handed it to Leslie.

She used the towel to wipe her eyes, then wrapped it around her hand. "I didn't wear it last night because it's a little too big. I think he was disappointed, but not as disappointed as he'll be when I tell him I lost it."

"I've never seen a man more smitten with a woman than

he is with you. As long as he knows you're in love with him, he won't let this bother him."

"That's kind of the problem. He doesn't know."

"You didn't tell him?"

"Not yet."

Hannah chuckled. "You never were one to rush into things."

No kidding. "What am I going to do?"

"You're going to get that ring out of the drain, and then you're going to call up that boy and tell him what he's waiting to hear."

"You make it so sound easy."

"And you're making it more difficult that it has to be."

Hannah was right. Now she just needed a plan. She'd call a plumber to get the ring out of the drain, and then she'd call Brent. Or would it be better to go see him in person? Yes, in person would be better.

She opened the phone book and flipped through the yellow pages till she found the listing for plumbers. She dialed the first number and let it ring. "Come on, come on," she said. "Pick up." Finally an answering machine gave her the company's business hours, then said to leave a message if there was an emergency and someone would return the call.

"Yes, this is an emergency," she said, practically shouting into the receiver. "I've dropped a ring down my kitchen sink and I have to get it out. Right away." She gave her name and phone number and hung up, then she dialed the next number.

An answering service told her the plumber wouldn't be available until Monday morning, and that if this was an emergency she should try the other plumbing company in town.

What to do? Under no circumstances could Brent find out about this. She had to find someone to get the ring out of there. She yanked open the cupboard doors and stared at the pipes under the sink. This didn't look anything like the plumbing at Brent's place and even if she knew what she was doing, she didn't have the right tools. She didn't have any tools.

But Nick did. Of course! If Brent could dismantle plumbing, so could her brother. She dialed his number and got his answering machine. "Doesn't *anybody* answer their phone on Sunday morning?" she said while she listened to his greeting.

"Nick? Hi, it's me, Leslie. I have a bit of a plumbing disaster and I need some help. Call me, okay?"

Where could he be this early on a Sunday morning? Probably at Maggie's. Did she dare call there? Given how few options she had, yes, she could.

Maggie seemed to be the only person in town who was answering her phone that morning, but Nick wasn't there. He was at their mother's place, helping to dismantle all the equipment from the party last night.

Of course he was. He'd volunteered to be in charge of the cleanup crew, and it would probably take them the better part of the day to take everything down and load it onto the trucks. That left her with two options. Wait till the plumber called, but that might not happen till tomorrow. Or call Brent, who was the only other person she knew who could take apart these stupid pipes.

Hannah had been watching and listening as she picked up the broken glass from the bottom of the sink. "Call him," she said.

What other choice did she have? She slowly dialed his number and waited.

"Good morning," he said. "Sleep well?"

"Not really." She might as well be honest.

"I'm sorry to hear that." He sounded detached, and that made her nervous.

"I didn't call to talk about how I slept."

"Why did you call?" Apparently he wasn't going to make this easy.

"I need your help."

"With?"

She closed her eyes and took a long, steadying breath. "I dropped something down the kitchen sink."

He laughed at that. "More diamonds down the drain?"

"No. It was…something else. I called both plumbers listed in the phone book but they're not available, and Nick is over at my mother's place. You're the only other person I know who can do this sort of thing."

"So I'm your last resort."

"No, you're not. I just didn't want you to think I'm a total klutz when it comes to jewelry and plumbing."

"Now where would I get an idea like that?"

Funny. "Will you come over? Please?"

"What have you lost this time?"

"I'd rather not say."

His silence was longer than she would have liked. "But it was a piece of jewelry," he said finally.

"What makes you ask that?"

"You just said you were a klutz when it comes to jewelry and plumbing."

Damn. She shouldn't have let that slip. "I said I didn't want you to think I was a klutz."

"Is this what they teach in law school?" he asked. "How to avoid answering a question?"

She sighed. This conversation was not going the way she'd hoped. "Okay. Fine. I dropped a piece of jewelry down the kitchen sink, and now I need your help to get it out."

He laughed softly. "See? That wasn't so hard. I'll be over in a few minutes."

She hung up and nodded at Hannah. "He's on his way."

"What did I tell you? Now let's get you in the bathroom and see how badly you cut yourself."

"I don't think it's too bad." But she could see where the blood had seeped through the towel, and the stain was getting bigger.

"You let me be the judge of that," Hannah said. "Do you have a first aid kit?"

"There's one in the bathroom."

She followed Hannah out of the kitchen and sat obediently on the lid of the toilet while the woman inspected the gash on her palm.

"It doesn't look that bad," she said.

Hannah agreed. "It's bad enough that it won't stop bleeding, but at least there's no glass in it. Just to be safe I think you should see a doctor. It might need a few stitches."

Leslie gritted her teeth as Hannah applied peroxide to the wound, then wrapped her hand with a gauze bandage. The doorbell rang just as they were finished.

Damn. She had planned to be dressed by the time he arrived.

"Good luck." Hannah gave her a broad smile and hurried down the hallway to her bedroom.

Leslie adjusted the sash on her dressing gown, stuck her injured hand behind her back and went to open the door.

BRENT HAD a hunch he knew what had gone down the drain. If it had been anything other than the ring he'd given her, she wouldn't have eliminated everyone else in town before she called him. On the bright side, the fact that it ended up in the plumbing suggested she had been wearing it, and confirmed his suspicion that it was a little too big. Which explained why she hadn't worn it last night, but not why she refused to say anything about it. Or about anything else, for that matter.

Then she opened the door and was standing there in a flimsy dressing gown that had him thinking that a piece of jewelry down the sink had simply been a ploy to get him over here. Except that didn't explain why her eyes were red and puffy, as though she'd been crying.

"Hi. It's in here," she said quietly, gesturing toward the kitchen.

"What happened to your hand?"

"Oh." She stuck it behind her back again. "It's not serious. I cut myself on the coffeepot I broke when I dropped my…something in the sink."

"It looks serious."

She shook her head. "I'll be fine."

"Did you put this bandage on it?"

"No, Hannah did."

"And she thinks it's fine?"

She hesitated.

"Why don't I just ask her myself," he said.

"Okay, fine. It's not that great. She thinks it might need a few stitches but that can wait till we find my…till we take the plumbing apart."

He now had no doubt whatsoever that it was his ring that had gone down the drain. And he shouldn't be pleased that it upset her so much, but after being given the cold shoulder last night and introduced as "a friend," he couldn't help thinking it was her turn to feel bad. When this latest plumbing disaster had been undone, he was going to install strainers in all the drains in this place. And his.

He followed her into the kitchen and set his toolbox on the floor. The amount of blood in the sink alarmed him but he didn't say anything. He opened the cupboard doors and was removing cleaning supplies when he realized she had a garbage disposal unit.

Oh, she was not going to be happy when she saw how easy this would be.

He unplugged the unit and rummaged for the flashlight in his toolbox.

Leslie stood beside him, watching intently.

He pushed down on the rubber flaps in the bottom of the sink and shone the flashlight down the drain. Yes, there it was, along with yesterday's coffee grounds, assorted vegetable peels and a couple of pieces of broken glass. He stuck his hand in as far as it would go, snagged the ring between two fingers and pulled it out.

Her eyes went wide. "You have got to be kidding me. *I* could have done that."

"Would you have shut off the power first?" He tossed his flashlight back in his toolbox and washed and dried his hands.

"Probably not."

"Then you might have been seeing the doctor for more than just a few stitches." He took her left hand and slid the ring on her finger. "Why didn't you tell me it was too big?"

"I wanted it to be perfect."

"Does everything have to be perfect?"

She looked at the ring on her hand, and then at him. "It is now."

He held her face in his hands and kissed her. "Is it okay for something to be the best it can be, without having to be perfect all the time?"

He was shocked to see her eyes fill with tears.

"I'm sorry," he said. "I didn't mean to make you cry."

"You didn't." She slid the ring off her finger and set it in a little glass dish on the counter next to the sink. "But you reminded me why I love you so much."

"What did you say?"

She put her arms around him. "I love you."

He lifted her onto the counter and positioned himself between her knees. Her arms stayed around him and he could feel the love in the way she kissed him.

"Where's Hannah?" he asked when she let him up for air.

"In her bedroom down the hall."

"So making love to you here on the kitchen counter is probably out of the question."

"Very much out of the question." She reached up to touch his hair, and winced. "I keep forgetting my hand."

"We need to get you to the clinic."

"I'll have to get dressed first."

She seemed in no hurry to move, though, so he slid a hand under her robe and up her leg. He groaned when he discovered just how undressed she really was. "You realize that letting you go now might actually kill me."

She laughed and inched herself a little closer. "After we've been married for a while, the novelty will wear off."

"Married? Yesterday you didn't want anyone to know we were engaged."

She adjusted herself so he had better access. "I changed my mind."

"People will talk."

"Since when do you care what other people think?"

"I don't, but I thought you did."

"I do. The people who matter aren't going to be the ones doing the talking." Her pupils were dark and dilated. "I think you'd better stop what you're doing."

"You're sending mixed messages."

She sighed and eased his hand from between her legs. "I'm good at that. Or bad, depending on how you look at it. But there's Hannah, and I guess I should see a doctor."

She held out her hand and he could see blood seeping through the gauze.

"Go get dressed," he said. "I'll drive."

She slid her arms around him and held on for a minute. "I didn't thank you last night for all the work you did."

"And I didn't tell you how proud I was of the job you did."

"I think it was because we were fighting."

"It didn't feel like a fight."

She smiled. "If you hadn't figured out how to get rid of Candice, there would have been a fight."

"You were jealous."

"Only if I thought you were falling for her womanly wiles."

"I was just being persuasive. That was your idea, not mine."

"Excuse me?"

"Did you see the amount on the check she wrote?"

Leslie shook her head.

"Let's just say, I can be *very* persuasive, too."

"Do you think she'll remember writing it?"

"I doubt it, so you should cash it before it bounces. But first you need to get dressed."

She kissed him. "I'm going," she said. She got as far as the doorway and came back. "I forgot something." She took her ring from the dish and handed it to him. "I've changed my mind about this being an engagement ring."

He felt like he'd been hit by a truck.

"You know, when the minister says, 'With this ring…'?"

Was it possible she would say what he hoped she was going to say?

"I want it to be with this one."

Yes, everything was possible.

*Turn the page for a sneak preview
of the first book in the new miniseries*
DIAMONDS DOWN UNDER
from Silhouette Desire®,
VOWS & A VENGEFUL GROOM
by Bronwyn Jameson

Available January 2008

Silhouette Desire®
Always Powerful, Passionate and Provocative

Kimberley Blackstone didn't notice the waiting horde of media until it was too late. Flashbulbs exploded around her like a New Year's light show. She skidded to a halt, so abruptly her trailing suitcase all but overtook her.

This had to be a case of mistaken identity. Surely. Kimberley hadn't been on the paparazzi hit list for close to a decade, not since she'd estranged herself from her billionaire father and his headline-hungry diamond business.

But no, it was *her* name they called. *Her* face was the focus of a swarm of lenses that circled her like avid hornets. Her heart started to pound with fear-fueled adrenaline.

What did they want?

What was going on?

With a rising sense of bewilderment she scanned the crowd for a clue, and her gaze fastened on a tall, leonine figure forcing his way to the front. A tall, familiar figure. Her head came up in stunned recognition, and their gazes collided across the sea of heads before the cameras erupted with another barrage of flashes, this time right in her exposed face.

Blinded by the flashbulbs—and by the shock of that momentary eye-meet—Kimberley didn't realize his intent until he'd forged his way to her side, possibly by the sheer strength of his personality. She felt his arm wrap around her shoulder, pulling her into the protective shelter of his body, allowing her no time to object. No chance to lift her hands to ward him off.

In the space of a hastily drawn breath, she found herself plastered knee-to-nose against six feet two inches of hard-bodied male.

Ric Perrini.

Her lover for ten torrid weeks, her husband for ten tumultuous days.

Her ex for ten tranquil years.

After all this time, he should not have felt so familiar but, oh dear, he did. She knew the scent of that body and its lean, muscular strength. She knew its heat and its slick power and every response it could draw from hers.

She also recognized the ease with which he'd taken control of the moment and the decisiveness of his deep voice when it rumbled close to her ear. "I have a car waiting outside. Is this your only luggage?"

Kimberley nodded. "I assume you will tell me," she said tightly, "what this welcome party is all about."

"Not while the welcome party is within earshot. No."

Barking a request for the cameramen to stand aside, Perrini took her hand and pulled her into step with his ground-eating stride. Kimberley let him, because he was right, damn his arrogant, Italian-suited hide. Despite the speed with which he whisked her across the airport terminal, she could almost feel the hot breath of the pursuing media on her back.

This was neither the time nor the place for explanations. Inside his car, however, she would get answers.

Now that the initial shock had been blown away—by the haste of their retreat, by the heat of her gathering indignation, by the rush of adrenaline fired by Perrini's presence and the looming verbal battle—her brain was starting to tick over. This had to be her father's doing. And if it was a Howard

Blackstone publicity ploy, then it had to be about Blackstone Diamonds, the company that ruled his life.

The knowledge made her chest tighten with a familiar ache of disillusionment.

She'd known her father would be flying in from Sydney for today's opening of the newest in his chain of exclusive, high-end jewelry boutiques. The opulent shopfront sat adjacent to the rival business where Kimberley worked. No coincidence, she thought bitterly, just as it was no coincidence that Ric Perrini was here in Auckland ushering her to his car.

Perrini was Howard Blackstone's right-hand man, second in command at Blackstone Diamonds, a legacy of his short-lived marriage to the boss's daughter. No doubt her father had sent him to fetch her; the question was *why?*

* * * * *

Get swept away down under with the glitz and glamour of the Blackstone empire as Kimberley tries to determine the real reason behind her "reunion" with Ric....

*Look for VOWS & A VENGEFUL GROOM
by Bronwyn Jameson,
in stores January 2008.*

When Kimberley Blackstone's father is
presumed dead, Kimberley is required to take
over the helm of Blackstone Diamonds. She
has to work closely with her ex, Ric Perrini, to
battle not only the press, but also the fierce
attraction still sizzling between them. Does Ric
feel the same...or is it the power her share of
Blackstone Diamonds will provide him as he
battles for boardroom supremacy.

Look for

VOWS &
A VENGEFUL GROOM

by

BRONWYN
JAMESON

Available January wherever you buy books

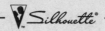

REQUEST YOUR FREE BOOKS!
2 FREE NOVELS PLUS 2
FREE GIFTS!

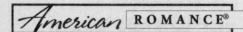 *American* | **ROMANCE**®

Heart, Home & Happiness!

YES! Please send me 2 FREE Harlequin American Romance® novels and my 2 FREE gifts. After receiving them, if I don't wish to receive any more books, I can return the shipping statement marked "cancel." If I don't cancel, I will receive 4 brand-new novels every month and be billed just $4.24 per book in the U.S., or $4.99 per book in Canada, plus 25¢ shipping and handling per book and applicable taxes, if any*. That's a savings of close to 15% off the cover price! I understand that accepting the 2 free books and gifts places me under no obligation to buy anything. I can always return a shipment and cancel at any time. Even if I never buy another book from Harlequin, the two free books and gifts are mine to keep forever.

154 HDN EEZK 354 HDN EEZV

Name _____ (PLEASE PRINT) _____

Address _____ Apt. # _____

City _____ State/Prov. _____ Zip/Postal Code _____

Signature (if under 18, a parent or guardian must sign)

Mail to the **Harlequin Reader Service**®:
IN U.S.A.: P.O. Box 1867, Buffalo, NY 14240-1867
IN CANADA: P.O. Box 609, Fort Erie, Ontario L2A 5X3

Not valid to current Harlequin American Romance subscribers.

Want to try two free books from another line?
Call 1-800-873-8635 or visit www.morefreebooks.com.

* Terms and prices subject to change without notice. NY residents add applicable sales tax. Canadian residents will be charged applicable provincial taxes and GST. This offer is limited to one order per household. All orders subject to approval. Credit or debit balances in a customer's account(s) may be offset by any other outstanding balance owed by or to the customer. Please allow 4 to 6 weeks for delivery.

Your Privacy: Harlequin is committed to protecting your privacy. Our Privacy Policy is available online at www.eHarlequin.com or upon request from the Reader Service. From time to time we make our lists of customers available to reputable firms who may have a product or service of interest to you. If you would prefer we not share your name and address, please check here. ☐

HAR07

nocturne™

Jachin Black always knew he was an outcast.
Not only was he a vampire, he was a vampire
banished from the Sanguinas society. Jachin, forced
to survive among mortals, is determined to buy
his way back into the clan one day.

Ariel Swanson, debut author of a vampire novel, could
be the ticket he needs to get revenge and take his
rightful place among the Sanguinas again. However,
the unsuspecting mortal woman has no idea of the
dark and sensual path she will be forced to travel.

Look for

RESURRECTION: THE BEGINNING

by

PATRICE MICHELLE

Available January 2008 wherever you buy books.

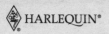

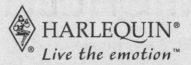

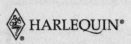

HARLEQUIN®

American ☆ Romance®

COMING NEXT MONTH

#1193 A RANDALL HERO by Judy Christenberry
When John Randall swerved to avoid a broken-down car on a deserted Rawhide,
Wyoming, road, the cowboy never dreamed he'd find a beautiful woman inside.
Like a knight without his steed, John came to her rescue. He had no choice.
Lucy Horton was on the run...and about to give birth.

#1194 FAMILY BY DESIGN by Roxann Delaney
Motherhood
Becca Tyler stomped on Nick Morelli's heart once—for all the wrong reasons.
Now the boy from the wrong side of the tracks is a successful builder, while the
high school golden girl is a single mom just scraping by. Although the spark of
their first love still glows, a secret Nick is keeping could ruin the lovers' reunion
before it begins....

#1195 GOOD HUSBAND MATERIAL by Kara Lennox
Fatherhood
The last thing Natalie Briggs needed in her hectic life was to run into her sexy
ex-husband at their twenty-fifth high school reunion! But when a romantic
night of lovemaking leads to an unexpected pregnancy, life gets even *more*
complicated. They split over child-related issues before...is this their second
chance to start a family?

#1196 EMMY AND THE BOSS by Penny McCusker
Nick Porter really hadn't wanted to hire an efficiency expert, but to secure a
bank loan to save his company, he had to put up with Emmy Jones. He was
expecting a suit-wearing, briefcase-toting uptight drill-sergeant type...Emmy
was anything but. Who knew an efficiency expert would come in such a pretty
package?

www.eHarlequin.com

HARCNM1207